Edmund Gosse

Firdausi in exile and other poems

Edmund Gosse

Firdausi in exile and other poems

ISBN/EAN: 9783743362659

Manufactured in Europe, USA, Canada, Australia, Japa

Cover: Foto ©Andreas Hilbeck / pixelio.de

Manufactured and distributed by brebook publishing software (www.brebook.com)

Edmund Gosse

Firdausi in exile and other poems

FIRDAUSI IN EXILE

AND OTHER POEMS

BY THE SAME AUTHOR.

IN VERSE.

On Viol and Flute : Lyrical Poems. 1873.
King Erik : a Tragedy. 1876.
New Poems. 1879.
The Masque of Painters. 1885.

IN PROSE.

Studies in the Literature of Northern Europe. 1879.
Gray. English Men of Letters Series. 1882.
Seventeenth Century Studies ; a contribution to the History
    of English Poetry. 1883.
From Shakespeare to Pope ; an Inquiry into the Causes
    and Development of the Classical School of English
    Poetry in the Seventeenth Century. 1885.

The Works of Thomas Gray. Edited, in four vols. 1884.

"*just outside Tampico a man-of-war was riding.*"

p. 36.

FIRDAUSI IN EXILE

AND

OTHER POEMS

BY

EDMUND GOSSE

LONDON

KEGAN PAUL, TRENCH & CO

MDCCCLXXXV

CONTENTS.

DEDICATION

TO

AUSTIN DOBSON.

*N*EIGHBOUR *of the near domain,*
   Stay awhile your passing wain!
Though to give is more your way,
Take a gift from me to-day!
From my homely store I bring
Signs of my poor husbanding;—
Here a spike of purple phlox,
Here a spicy bunch of stocks,
Mushrooms from my moister fields,
Apples that my orchard yields,—
Nothing,—for the show they make,
Something,—for the donor's sake;
Since for ten years we have been
Best of neighbours ever seen;

We have fronted evil weather,
Nip of critic's frost, together ;
We have shared laborious days,
Shared the pleasantness of praise ;
Brother not more kind to brother,
We have cheered and helped each other ;
Till so far the fields of each
Into the other's stretch and reach,
That perchance when both are gone
Neither may be named alone.

FIRDAUSI IN EXILE.[1]

FIRDAUSI IN EXILE.

I.

NOW God who flames the buckler of the sun,
    And lights that lamp of heaven, the glorious moon
In the proud breast of Mahmoud had begun
    To stir remorse, and, like the loud typhoon,
Shame blew his thoughts in gusts about his soul,
    Remembering that old man whose sandy shoon
Pressed the low shores where distant waters roll.
    And all his wrongs, and unrequited boon.

II.

Since, greatest poet whom the world contains,
    Firdausi, on whose tongue the sweet Fársí
Sounded like whispering leafage when it rains,
    Who loved the ancient kings, and learned to see

Their buried shapes in vision one by one,
  And wove their deeds in lovely minstrelsy,
For all the glory that his name had won
  To Persia, was in exile by the sea.

III.

In vain through sixty thousand verses clear
  He sang of feuds and battles, friend and foe,
Of the frail heart of Kaous, spent with fear,
  And Kai Khosrau who vanished in the snow,
And white-haired Zal who won the secret love
  Of Rudabeh where water-lilies blow,
And lordliest Rustem, armed by gods above
  With every power and virtue mortals know.

IV.

In vain these stories of the godlike kings,
  Whose bodies were as brass, their hearts as fire,
This verse that centuries with wasting wings
  Will never harm, though men with gods conspire—

In vain the good Firdausi, full of years,
  Inscribed this treasure to his Shah's desire ;
For Mahmoud, heedless of the poet's tears,
  Forgot his oath, nor gave the promised hire.

V.

For each sonorous verse one piece of gold :
  Such was the promise that the Shah had made,
But when the glorious perfect tale was told,
  The file of laden elephants delayed ;
For Hasan, that black demon, held the car
  Of Mahmoud, and spoke tenderly, and said,
" The end of this old man, my lord, is near ;
  For gold let silver in the sacks be weighed."

VI.

Thereat Firdausi, when it came, was wroth,
  And being within the bath, where all might see,
Called the two serving-men, and bid them both
  Divide the silver for their service-fee,

And told Ayaz, the false Shah's chamberlain,
   " Returning to thy master, say from me,
'Twas not for silver that I toiled amain
   And wove my verse for thirty years and three."

VII.

Then round him came his friends and bade him fly
   From Mahmoud's vengeance, and the murderous sword;
But he, being placable of heart, would try
   For peace, since enmity his soul abhorred;
So in the garden where the Shah was used
   To breathe the spice that many a rose outpoured,
Firdausi met his master as he mused,
   And bowed down at his feet without a word.

VIII.

Yet grudging was the pardon, faint the smile,
   And when that evening in the mosque he lay,
A veiled dervish, muttering all the while,
   Crept near Firdausi, while he seemed to pray,

And whispered, " Fly from Ghaznin, fly to-night,
  The bowstring waits for thee at break of day ;
Thou shalt not 'scape because thy beard is white—
  Begone ! " and like a snake he slipped away.

IX.

Then, when of worship there was made an end,
  Firdausi rolled his prayer-mat up, and turned
To that bright niche where all believers bend,
  And by the light of lamps that round him burned
Wrote on a blue tile with a diamond point
  Two couplets that may yet be well discerned,
Though all the mosque be crumbling joint from joint,
  By long decay and mouldering age inurned :

X.

" The happy court of Mahmoud is a sea,
  A sea of endless waves without a coast ;
In my unlucky star the fault must be
  If I who plunged for pearls in it am lost."

Then to his house he went, weary and sad,
  And called around him those who loved him most,
And gave them all the treasure that he had,
  Soft silken raiment that a king might boast.

XI.

But in a saintly gaberdine set out
  And crossed the moonlit streets, and left the town,
Nor stopped to hear the lonely owlet shout
  His dreamy menace from the turret's crown,
But where the cypresses and myrtles hoar
  Hid the white house of Ayaz, stooping down,
He thrust a letter underneath the door,
  And faded in the shadow broad and brown.

XII.

That letter bade the chamberlain beloved
  Before the dawn to seek his master's face,
And plead until his blandishments had moved
  The Shah to grant him twenty days of grace;

In twenty days a paper folded fair

    Should Ayaz in his master's fingers place,

Which to the gracious Sultan would declare

    Firdausi's secret wish, and plead his case.

XIII.

The Sultan vowed : but for those twenty-days

    The Sultan yawned upon his peacock-throne ;

The rebeck and the Turkish minstrel's lays

    With their sweet treble jarred him to the bone.

All night he tossed in fever, all day long

    Far from his blithe hareem he paced alone,

Or scowled to hear the trampling and the song

    Where down the cool bazaar the lanterns shone.

XIV.

At last, at last the twentieth morning broke,

    And Mahmoud, flushed with pleasure, rose and cried

For fair Ayaz, who from his slumber woke,

    And brought the sealèd letter, white and wide.

In Allah's name the Sultan broke the seal ;
  His long-pent wishes satisfied, he sighed,
But reading on, he stared, and seemed to reel,
  And crushed the leaf, and gazed out stony-eyed.

XV.

It was that scathing satire, writ in fire,
  And music such as the red tiger makes
Over a man, the food of her desire,
  When she lies down among the crested brakes—
That satire which the world still shudders at,
  Whose cadence in the hearer's sense still aches,
At bare recital of whose singing hate
  The conscience of forgetful kings awakes.

XVI.

"O Mahmoud, of the whole world conqueror,
  You fear not me?—fear God !" The Sultan fell
With outstretched arms before the chamber door,
  Ashen with rage, and his breast's heave and swell

Was like an earthquake ; no word passed his lips,
  But curses from the foulest pit of hell,
Till evening brought his soul through that eclipse,
  And he rose up, and drank, and feasted well.

XVII.

But old Firdausi, bearing eastward still,
  Through many a Tartar camp, his woven mat,
At last, one evening, climbed a scarpèd hill
  From whence he saw the white roofs of Herat :
Downward he passed, and in a garden, sweet
  With roses and narcissus, down he sat,
And wondered if his mountain-weary feet
  Might dare to rest where earth was smooth and flat.

XVIII.

Then suddenly his tired eyes laughed at last,
  For he remembered, by the gift of fate,
Where once he lodged in merry days long past
  At Herat, in the arch above the gate.

There Abou'lmaani sold his ancient books,
    A man discreet and old, without a mate,
And there Firdausi oft, in dusty nooks,
    Had chanted verses till the night was late.

XIX.

To Abou'lmaani in the dusk he went,
    And found him still more wrinkled than of yore,
An owlish figure, angular and bent,
    But hearty still and honest to the core.
So there among the rolls of parchment sere
    Once more he drank the mystic Dikhan lore,
But never sought the daylight streets, for fear
    Of treachery, and the hatred Mahmoud bore.

XX.

And little rest he had, and brief delight,
    For rumours from the court at Ghaznin ran,
And with a short farewell he fled by night
    Across the mountains to the Caspian ;

A gentle Sultan ruled from Astrabad
   The jasmine-gardens of Mazinderan,
And to his little court, humble and sad,
   One morning came a white-haired minstrel-man.

XXI.

Like parrots, one and all, with shrieking tongues
   The poets knew their lord, and screamed his name,
Bitter with hate ; but his sweet learned songs
   Had touched the Sultan with their sacred flame ;
He bade the jealous poets all make way,
   And did Firdausi honour to their shame,
And asked by what fair accident that day
   From stately Ghaznin such a stranger came.

XXII.

But when he knew, and heard of Mahmoud's rage,
   He trembled, and his fingers stroked his beard ;
For scarcely could his pastoral province wage
   Safe war with one whom all the nations feared ;

So blushing much, as one who loathes his task,
　　He bade his guest, whom meat and wine had cheered,
To grant the boon that he could scarcely ask
　　Of one so deeply loved, so long revered.

XXIII.

Firdausi rose and sighed, and went his way,
　　But ere he reached the gate of Astrabad,
The Sultan sent three men in rich array
　　Laden with gifts, the lordliest that he had,
And camels, that the bard might ride at ease,
　　And lutes, and a Circassian serving-lad ;
So after many days he passed with these
　　Far down the lordly Tigris to Baghdad.

XXIV.

Here underneath the palm-trees, full of shade,
　　The poet tasted peace, and lingered long ;
The Master of the Faithful he obeyed,
　　And searched the Koran for a theme for song.

The vizier lodged him in his own fair house,
 Where wise men gathered in a learned throng,
And when the Khalif heard his pious vows,
 He gave him gifts and shielded him from wrong.

XXV.

There in a white-walled garden full of trees,
 Through which there ran a deep cold water-brook
Fringed with white tulips and anemones,
 Among the tender grass he wrote the book
Of Yousouf and Zuleika; not one word
 Was there of all the windy war that shook
Iran of old, nor was the ear once stirred
 With any name the Faithful might rebuke.

XXVI.

Nine thousand Persian verses told the tale,
 And when the perfect poem was set down,
He rose, and left the plaintive nightingale
 That long had tuned her throat to his sweet moan;

Before the Khalif on a broad divan,
  To sound of rebecks, in a silken gown,
He sat in state, and when the dance began
  Declaimed aloud that song of high renown.

XXVII.

Its music sank on well-attempered ears ;
  The Khalif lounged upon his throne, and cried,
"Lo ! I this day am as a man who hears
  The angel Gabriel murmur at his side—
And dies not." At the viewless hareem-door
  The screen was swayed by bending forms that sighed,
And scheikhs and soldiers, young and old, for more
  Still pressed and wished, and scarce would be denied.

XXVIII.

Ah, palmy days were those for singer's craft !
  Now every worldling flings his cap in rhyme,
And from an easy bow lets fly a shaft
  At verse much honoured in his grandsire's time ;

Now many a ghazel, soft with spices, trips
  Along the alien mouth with frivolous chime,
And lightly rises from unhonoured lips
  The ancient rhythm sonorous and sublime.

XXIX.

But great Firdausi met with honour then,
  Garments and jewels, and much store of gold ;
Till one, the basest and the worst of men,
  Rode out by stealth that Hasan might be told
Who, when he heard in Ghaznin that his foe
  Sat, robed and glorious, as he sat of old,
Stirred up with whispers to a fiery glow
  The rage of Mahmoud, which was wellnigh cold.

XXX.

So Mahmoud sent to Baghdad embassies
  Demanding speedily Firdausi's head,
Or else the town among her ancient trees
  Must look for instant war, the missive said ;

C

The stately Khalif rose in wrath and pride,
    And swore that till each faithful heart was dead,
His hospitable sword should leave his side,
    And rolling Tigris blush in Persian red.

XXXI.

But ere the messengers with garments rent
    Fled back to Ghaznin at the trumpet's blare,
Firdausi to the warlike Khalif sent
    His little servant with the flowing hair,
Who scarcely knowing what he said, by rote
    Repeated, "Master, have no thought or care
Of old Firdausi; he can dive and float
    A fish in water and a bird in air.

XXXII.

"The quail upon the mountain needs no host
    To guard her covert in the waving grass;
And though Mahmoud and all his ships be tost
    On lake or sea, the little trout will pass.

Stain not thy sword for such a guest as I,

    For God, before whose sight man's heart is glass,

Will see the stain that on my soul will lie

    If life-blood gush from helmet or cuirass.

XXXIII.

" I go my way into the lion's mouth,

    And as I journey, God will hold my hand ;

Whether I wander north or wander south,

    There is no rest for me in any land ;

The serpent's fang will find me though I fly

    To Frankistan, or Ind, or Samarkand ;

I will go home again, for tired am I,

    And ail too old to wrestle and withstand.

XXXIV.

" So send the Persian envoys back in peace,

    For, whilst these words are spoken, I am gone ;

Though thou shouldst scour the lands and drain the seas,

    Thou shalt not find me, since I wend alone ;

For all the days that I have loved thee well
  My heart is myrrh, that kindles at thy throne,
And I am sadder than my tongue can tell,
  That I must leave thee with the end unknown."

XXXV.

So with a single camel, clad to sight
  Like some poor merchant of the common sort,
Firdausi left the town at morning light,
  And passed the gate, and passed the sullen fort,
Unnoted ; and his face was to the east,
  Towards Hasan and the hateful Persian court,
As if contempt of life were in his breast,
  And loathing of his days, so sad and short.

XXXVI.

But sure some angel had forewarned him well,
  And murmured in his ear the name of " home ; "
For through this perilous journey there befell
  No evil wheresoever he might come ;

And Mahmoud guessed not that the foe he sought
   Had turned upon his track and ceased to roam,
But sent out scouts, and bade his head be brought
   From Bahrein by the vexed Arabian foam.

XXXVII.

At last one night, as lone Firdausi rode,
   The dawn broke grey across the starry sky,
And far ahead behind the mountains flowed
   A sudden gush of molten gold on high ;
The glory spread from snowy horn to horn,
   Tinged by the rushing dawn with sanguine dye,
And Tous, the little town where he was born,
   Flashed at his feet, with white roofs clustered nigh.

XXXVIII.

His aged sister fell upon his neck ;
   His girl, his only child, with happy tears,
Clung to his knees, and sobbing, with no check
   Poured out the story of her hopes and fears.

Gravely his servants gave him welcome meet,

 And when his coming reached the townfolk's ears

They ran to cluster round him in the street,

 And gave him honour for his wealth of years.

XXXIX.

And there in peace he waited for the end ;

 But in all distant lands where Mahmoud sent,

Each Prince and Sultan was Firdausi's friend,

 And murmured, like a high-stringed instrument

Swept by harsh fingers, at a quest so rude,

 And chid the zeal, austere and violent,

That drove so sweet a voice to solitude,

 And bade the Shah consider and relent.

XL.

And once from Delhi, that o'erhangs the tide

 Of reedy Ganges like a gorgeous cloud,

The Hindu king, with Persia close allied,

 Sent letters larger than the faith he vowed,

Smelling of sandalwood and ambergris,
　And cited from Firdausi lines that showed
Friendship should be eternal, and the bliss
　Of love a gift to make a master proud.

XLI.

So while these words were fresh in Mahmoud's brain
　He went one night into the mosque to pray,
And by the swinging lamp deciphered plain
　The verse Firdausi, ere he fled away,
Wrote on the wall; and one by one there rose
　Sad thoughts and sweet of many a vanished day,
When his soul hovered on the measured close
　And wave-beat of the rich heroic lay.

XLII.

Mourning the verse, he mourned the poet too;
　And he who oftentimes had lain awake
Long nights in wide-eyed vision to pursue
　His victim, yearning in revengeful ache,

Forgot all dreams of a luxurious death
    By trampling elephant or strangling snake,
And thought on his old friend with tightened breath,
    And flushed, remorseful for his anger's sake.

XLIII.

Back to his court he went, molten at heart,
    And all his rage on faithless Hasan turned ;
For when he thought him of that tongue's black art,
    His wrath was in him like a coal that burned ;
He bade his several ministers appear
    Before his throne, and by inquiry learned
The cunning treason of the false vizier,
    And all his soul's deformity discerned.

XLIV.

Hasan was slain that night ; and of the gold
    His monkey-hands had thieved from rich and poor,
The Sultan bade the money should be told
    Long due as payment at Firdausi's door ;

But when the sacks of red dinars were full,
  Mahmoud bethought him long, and pondered sore,
Since vainly any king is bountiful
  Not knowing where to seek his creditor.

XLV.

But while he fretted at this ignorance,
  A dervish came to Ghaznin, who had seen,
In passing through the streets of Tous, by chance
  Firdausi in his garden cool and green ;
At this Mahmoud rejoiced, and, with glad eyes
  Swimming in tears, quivering with liquid sheen,
Wrote words of pardon, and in welcoming wise
  Prayed all might be again as all had been.

XLVI.

But while Firdausi brooded on his wrong,
  One day he heard a child's clear voice repeat
The bitter jibe of his own scathing song ;
  Whereat he started, and his full heart beat

Its last deep throb of agony and rage ;
　　And blinded in sharp pain, with tottering feet,
Being very feeble in extremest age,
　　He fell, and died there in the crowded street.

XLVII.

The light of three-and-fourscore summers' suns
　　Had blanched the silken locks round that vast brow ;
If Mahmoud might have looked upon him once,
　　He would have bowed before him meek and low ;
The majesty of death was in his face,
　　And those wide waxen temples seem to glow
With morning glory from some holy place
　　Where angels met him in a burning row.

XLVIII.

His work was done ; the palaces of kings
　　Fade in long rains, and in loud earthquakes fall ;
The poem that a godlike poet sings
　　Shines o'er his memory like a brazen wall ;

No suns may blast it, and no tempest wreck,
   Its periods ring above the trumpet's call,
Wars and the tumult of the sword may shake,
   And may eclipse it—it survives them all.

XLIX.

Now all this while along the mountain road
   The mighty line of camels wound in state ;
Shuddering they moved beneath their massy load,
   And swinging slowly with the balanced weight ;
Burden of gold, and garments red as flame,
   They bore, not dreaming of the stroke of fate,
And so at last one day to Tous they came
   And entered blithely at the eastern gate.

L.

But in the thronged and noiseless streets they found
   All mute, and marvelled at the tears men shed,
And no one asked them whither they were bound,
   And when, for very shame discomfited,

They cried, " Now tell us where Firdausi lies ! "
   A young man like a cypress rose and said—
The anger burning in his large dark eyes—
   "Too late Mahmoud remembers ! He is dead !

LI.

"Speed ! haste away ! hie to the western port ;
   Perchance the convoy has not passed it yet !
But hasten, hasten, for the hour is short,
   And your short-memoried master may forget !
Behold, they bear Firdausi to the tomb,
   Pour in his open grave your golden debt !
Speed ! haste ! and with the treasures of the loom
   Dry the sad cheeks where filial tears are wet !

LII.

" Lead your bright-harnessed camels one by one,
   The dead man journeys, and he fain would ride ;
Pour out your unctuous perfumes in the sun,
   The rose has spilt her petals at his side ;

Your citherns and your carven rebecks hold
  Here when the nightingale untimely died,
And ye have waited well till he is cold,
  Now wrap his body in your tigers' hide."

LIII.

And so the young man ceased ; but one arose
  Of graver aspect, not less sad than he.
" Nay, let," he cried, " the sunshine and the snows
  His glittering gold and silk-soft raiment be ;
Approach not with unhallowed steps profane
  The low white wall, the shadowy lotus-tree ;
Nor let a music louder than the rain
  Disturb him dreaming through eternity.

LIV.

" For him no more the dawn will break in blood,
  No more the silver moon bring fear by night ;
He starts no longer at a tyrant's mood,
  Serene for ever in the Prophet's sight ;

The soul of Yaman breathed on him from heaven,

And he is victor in the unequal fight ;

To Mahmoud rage and deep remorse are given,

To old Firdausi rest and long delight."

THE CRUISE OF THE
"ROVER."[2]

I.

THEY sailed away one morning when sowing-time
was over,

  In long red fields above the sea they left the sleeping
wheat ;

Twice twenty men of Devonshire who manned their ship
the *Rover*,

  Below the little busy town where all the schooners
meet.

II.

Their sweethearts came and waved to them, and filled
with noise of laughter

  The echoing port below the cliff where thirty craft can
ride ;

D

Each lad cried out, "Farewell to thee!" the captain
    shouted after,
  "By God's help we'll be back again before the harvest-
    tide."

III.

They turned the Start and slipped along with speedy
    wind and weather;
  Passed white Terceira's battlements, and, close upon
    the line,
Ran down a little carrack full of cloth and silk and
    leather,
  And golden Popish images and good Madeira wine.

IV.

The crew with tears and curses went tacking back to
    Flores;
  The English forty cut the seas where none before had
    been,

And spent the sultry purple nights in English songs, and
    stories
  Of England, and her soldiers, and her Spaniard-hating
    queen.

V.

At last the trade-wind caught them, the pale sharks reeled
    before them,
  The little *Rover* shot ahead across the western seas ;
All night the larger compass of a tropic sky passed o'er
    them,
  Till they won the Mexique waters through a strait of
    banyan-trees.

VI.

And there good luck befel them, for divers times they
    sighted
  The sails of Spanish merchantmen bound homeward
    with their wares ;

And twice they failed to follow them, and once they
    stopped benighted ;
  But thrice the flag of truce flew out, and the scented
    prize was theirs.

VII.

But midsummer was on them, with close-reef gales and
    thunder,
  Their heavy vessel wallowed beneath her weight of
    gold ;
A long highway of ocean kept them and home
    asunder,
  So back they turned towards England with a richly-
    laden hold.

VIII.

But just outside Tampico a man-of-war was riding,
  And all the mad young English blood in forty brains
    awoke,

The *Rover* chased the monster, and swiftly shorewards
gliding,

Dipped down beneath the cannonade that o'er her
bulwarks broke.

IX.

Three several days they fought her, and pressed her till
she grounded

On the sandy isle of Carmen, where milky palm-trees
grow ;

Whereat she waved an ensign, a peaceful trumpet
sounded,

And all the Spaniards cried for truce, surrendering in a
row.

X.

Alas ! the wiles and jesuitries of scoundrel-hearted
Spaniards,

The scarlet woman dyes their hands in deeper red than
hers,

For every scrap of white that decked their tackling and
　　their lanyards
　Just proved them sly like devils and cowardly like
　　curs.

XI.

For out from countless coverts, from low palm-shaded
　　islands,
　That fledged in seeming innocence the smooth and
　　shining main,
The pinnaces came gliding and hemmed them round in
　　silence,
　All manned with Indian bravos and whiskered dogs of
　　Spain.

XII.

The captain darted forwards, his fair hair streamed
　　behind him,
　He shouted in his cheery voice, "For home and for
　　the Queen!"

Three times he waved his gallant sword, but the flashes
  seemed to blind him,
  And a hard look came across his mouth where late a
  smile had been.

XIII.

We levelled with our muskets, and the foremost boat
  went under,
  The ship's boy seized a trumpet and blew a merry
  blast ;
The Spanish rats held off a while, and gazed at us in
  wonder,
  But the hindmost pushed the foremost on, and boarded
  us at last.

XIV.

They climbed the larboard quarter with their hatchets and
  their sabres ;
  The Devon lads shot fast and hard, and sank their
  second boat,

But the Popish hordes were legion, and Hercules his
labours
   Are light beside the task to keep a riddled barque
   afloat.

XV.

And twenty men had fallen, and the *Rover's* deck was
reeling,
   And the brave young captain died in shouting loud
   " Elizabeth ! "
The Spaniards dragged the rest away just while the ship
was heeling,
   Lest she should sink and rob them of her sailors'
   tortured breath.

XVI.

For they destined them to perish in a slow and cruel
slaughter,
   A feast for monks and Jesuits too exquisite to lose ;

So they caught the English sailors as they leaped into the
water,

And a troop of horse as convoy brought them north to
Vera Cruz.

XVII.

They led them up a sparkling beach of burning sand and
coral,

They dragged the brave young Englishmen like hounds
within a leash ;

They passed beneath an open wood of leaves that smelt of
laurel,

Bound close together, each to each, with cords that cut
the flesh.

XVIII.

And miles and miles along the coast they tramped beneath
no cover,

Till in their mouths each rattling tongue was like a
hard dry seed,

And ere they came to Vera Cruz when that long day was
   over,
   The coral cut their shoes to rags, and made them wince
      and bleed.

XIX.

Then as they clambered up the town, the jeering crowd
   grew thicker,
   And laughed to see their swollen feet and figures
      marred and bent,
And women with their hair unloosed stood underneath
   the flicker
   Of torch and swinging lantern, and cursed them as they
      went.

XX.

And three men died of weariness before they reached the
   prison,
   And one fell shrieking with the pain of a poniard in the
      back,

And when dawn broke in the morning three other souls
    had risen
  To bear the dear Lord witness of the hellish Spaniard
    pack.

XXI.

But the monks girt up their garments, the friars bound
    their sandals,
  They hurried to the market-place with faggots of dry
    wood,
And the acolytes came singing, with their incense and
    their candles,
  To offer to their images a sacrifice of blood.

XXII.

But they sent the leech to tend them, with his pouch and
    his long phial,
  And the Jesuits came smiling, with honied words at
    first,

For they dared not burn the heretics without some show
of trial,
  And the English lads were dying of poisoned air and
thirst.

XXIII.

So they gave them draughts of water from a great cold
earthen firkin,
  And brought them to the courtyard where the tall
hidalgo sat,
And he looked a gallant fellow in his boots and his rough
jerkin,
  With the jewels on his fingers, and the feather in his
hat.

XXIV.

And he spoke out like a soldier, for he said, " Ye caught
them fighting,
  They met you with the musket, by the musket they
shall fall,

They are Christians in some fashion, and the pile you're
bent on lighting
    Shall blaze with none but Indians, or it shall not blaze
at all."

XXV.

So they led them to a clearing in the wood outside the
city,
    Struck off the gyves that bound them, and freed each
crippled hand,
And dark-eyed women clustered round and murmured in
their pity,
    But won no glance nor answer from the steadfast
English band.

XXVI.

For their lives rose up before them in crystalline com-
pleteness,
    And they lost the flashing soldiery, the sable horde of
Rome,

And the great magnolias round them, with wave on wave
    of sweetness,
  Seemed just the fresh profusion and hawthorn lanes of
    home.

XXVII.

They thought about the harvests, and wondered who
    would reap them ;
  They thought about the little port where thirty craft
    can ride ;
They thought about their sweethearts, and prayed the
    Lord to keep them ;
  Then kissed each other silently, and hand in hand they
    died.

THE ISLAND OF THE
BLEST. [5]

THE ISLAND OF THE BLEST.

A variation on an old theme.

I.

THREE days beneath that hurrying storm we flew,
  With eyes that ached within the flashing gloom,
With ears that, muffled in our mantles, knew
  The shriek and clangour of the whistling spume,
  With hearts that ceased to quail at any doom ;
No respite had we for one moment's space,
  But heard the winds pipe and the waters boom,
Nor through the darkness saw a kindly face,
Nor dared to let one hand a brother's hand enlace.

II.

Till, the fourth morn, when from a swoon we waked,
  Around us lay a cool and quiet sea,

E

Ringed by a dead grey sky enstarred and flaked

   With cloudlets still as any cloud can be,

   All pointing, like trim pennons, to our lee,

Where broke a light on the horizon dim,

   So soft and luminous and deep that we,

Like men from shipwreck saved, pealed forth a hymn

To that first gracious Good that saved us, life and limb.

III.

Towards this fair light our helm we would have set,

   But that the compass of our ship was crazed,

For that strange storm had taught it to forget,

   And round from south to north it quivered, dazed ;

   But brighter that great lamp of dawning blazed,

And of herself our bark turned round her head,

   And onward every weary seaman gazed,

As o'er the opal glistening wave we fled,

And marked an island rise out of the ocean-bed.

IV.

A craggy isle it seemed, of wanton shape,
  Rounded with woodland, scarped by peaks on high,
With many a curve of brave fantastic cape,
  And bright bare ridge of rock against the sky ;
  Straight towards it less we seemed to float than fly,
Like those swift barks that spread their ample sail
  To catch the side-winds as they wander by
O'er Russian lakes when frosty moons prevail,
And skim the shining flats before an icy gale.

V.

But ever as we neared that land of light
  An odour broke upon our ravished sense,
A mingled perfume deep and exquisite
  More cool and soft than burnèd frankincense,—
  Like many a summer flower, but more intense,
The thrilling jonquil, the rich rose, were there,
  The tender smell of a thick myrtle-fence,
Scents of young grapes, and budding leaves, and air
Through which from dawn to dusk the hurrying bees repair.

VI.

And breathing deeply of this atmosphere,
    We smiled, and gazed each on his comrade's face,
And found the skin that was so parched and sere
    Had straight recovered each accustomed grace,
    As if our feet stood on some holy place ;
Though we had toiled so long upon the deep,
    And all grown old and worn in piteous case,
That odour fine had cleared our eyes like sleep,
And smoothed our faded hair and taught our hearts to leap.

VII.

And now beneath the magic isle we came ;
    Full of fair havens was it, blue and wide,
With iron promontories fit to tame
    The wildest storm and make a calm inside,
    Where gentlest birds might plume themselves and ride ;
White cities nestled under every hill,
    Stretching their marble feet to touch the tide,
And shallops driven by more than mortal skill,
Meandered here and there, or cleft the wave at will.

VIII.

Down coverts thick with cedar and with pine
    Sonorous waters dropt their silver shafts,
And through the woods we saw the temples shine,
    Around whose portals many a priestess wafts
    The incense of the island's handicrafts ;
The morning broke upon a people's prayer,
    We drank the odorous wind in deeper draughts,
And seeing the land so pure and void of care,
Our very hearts were touched, and we grew gentle there.

IX.

Meanwhile our helmless vessel cleft the sea,
    Following, we knew not how, the piercing sound
Of some high flute or pipe that seemed to be
    Blown by a mouth beyond the utmost bound
    Of this sweet island that our fate had found ;
At last we neared a headland grey and hoary,
    And like a living thing our ship veered round,
Past the firm granite of that promontory
Into a bay profound that flashed with light and glory.

X.

We shot to right and left amid a fleet
    Of ships of fairy trim and build antique ;
Until below a stately marble street
    Our prow against the quay began to shriek ;
      The forms that crowded round us all were Greek,
Yet by some marvel of the shifty brain
      Their tongue seemed ours when they began to speak,
And ours seemed theirs when we replied again,
And words fell thick and fast in showers like summer rain.

XI.

For these grave strangers marvelled at our dress,
    Our Northern faces and our wondrous ship,
And more and more around us all would press,
    Nor let us from their curious questioning slip,
      And weighed our answers, lest our tongues should trip ;
Nor could our smiles and honied speech assuage
      The darkening eye and lip on hard-pressed lip,
They doubted lest our band had come to wage
Fell war with sylvan peace, their island-heritage.

XII.

So for a while they whispered in a ring,

  Taking deep counsel in their urgent case,

Then seemed to judge that none beside their king

  Could truly tell if we were brave or base,

  Then, child-like, said so to our very face,

And then with many a threat of pains and blows,

  In quaint procession led us from that place,

Bound three by three in chaplets of wild rose,

Since no severer chain that happy island knows.

XIII.

Far up the hot white streets of their great town,

  Past cool arcades well-trellised round with vines,

Our genial captors, feigning many a frown,

  Conducted us, and by their words and signs

  Would fain have had us dread their deep designs ;

We smiled and nimbly followed, as seemed best,

  Till soon, beneath some solitary pines,

We halted meekly at their chief's behest,

And learned their land was named the "Island of the

    Blest."

XIV.

Then while we rested there, he taught us, too,
    That Cretan Rhadamanthus was their king,
And that before his judgment-seat he drew
    All that offended right in anything,
    Or had a question of the law to bring ;
Then we and they arose again, and sought
    The highway where the parched cicalas sing,
And while we went, our courteous leader taught
The order of that state to us with minds distraught.

XV.

But when at last before the King we stood
    Deep in a temple built above the town,
After some brief delay we understood
    Three cases must be tried before our own,
    Whereat our captors, smiling, sat them down,
And we, in patience, watched that bright-eyed king
    Stroke his white beard and shake his massy crown,
And saw the swift obsequious usher bring
The persons of each suit together in a ring.

XVI.

But first a soldier of heroic mould

    Threw on each side the pressing populace ;

He wore a bright cuirass of beaten gold,

    Fitting the captain of a kingly race,

    But there was madness stamped upon his face ;

Up to the throne he darted and stood still,

    A monument of shattered power and grace,

Shouting, "I am Telamonian Ajax !   Will,

O King, that I my place among my peers should fill !"

XVII.

And Rhadamanthus bowed above his beard ;

    And some came forth who of Cassandra spake,

And of his own mad death ; but all men feared

    Those wandering eyes and lip-line like a snake ;

    Nor loved an answer from his lips to take ;

So, after many words, the King decreed,

    That he his thirst with hellebore should slake,

And after, in the bath awhile should bleed,

Till the great leech of Cos pronounced him sane indeed.

XVIII.

Then, loudly wrangling, in the court upsprung
    Theseus and Menelaus ; by their side
Came Helen blushing ; to her maids she clung.
    But let her purple eyes roll far and wide,
      And watched the monarch while her cause was tried ;
Since each would have her for his wife, yet she
    Her lovely hand to neither had denied,
Nor blushed she when the King's supreme decree
To Menelaus gave her loveliness in fee.

XIX.

And close to us their bright procession swept,
    As Atreus' son led off his beauteous prize,
But Theseus glowered as one who would have wept,
    Had not his pride sealed fast his iron eyes ;
      Slowly he rose, burdened with many sighs,
While down the steps he watched her twinkling feet,
    Then, like a warrior just before he dies,
Wrapped close his mantle round his heart's defeat,
And vanished like a ghost far down the glittering street.

XX.

Then Hannibal with Alexander strove

 For precedence, and many a cunning saw

Each quoted to the King, who dreamed above

 Like some old incarnation of the law ;

 His judgment, like a lot, we saw him draw,

And he that conquered India proudly won ;

 The other knew that judgment had no flaw,

And like a sulky lion sought the sun,

While Rhadamanthus turned and eyed us one by one.

XXI.

There in a group our crew together stood,

 Whispering light whimsies or fantastic quips,

All fellows of the same quaint brotherhood,

 Pale Vannus mourning still time's long eclipse ;

 And bearded Paradox, with laughing lips,

Murmuring strange verses ;—Bion, like a wind,

 Thin, dark and keen, whose speech so nimbly trips

That, like the hart, it leaves pursuit behind ;—

And gentlest Horace swayed by his uncertain mind.

XXII.

And many more were there ; to whom, struck dumb
   By all his majesty, the judge began :—
"Say who and from what unknown realm ye come,
   To us who never yet saw living man?
   Long years ago our feverish mortal span
Was ended, and this sacred land is given
   To us, a little, but immortal clan,
From whom the bands of fleshly birth are riven,
Who know no life nor death, and taste nor hell nor heaven.

XXIII.

"Ye men in whom the pulse of life yet runs
   Have nought to do with us or we with you ;
We envy not your swift-revolving suns,
   Your headstrong hopes and summers cold and few.
   Frail, captious creatures are ye, who pursue
An aim we know to be too high for us ;
   When all the world is yours to battle through,
Why come ye, strangers, uninvited thus,
Of our unsullied peace so coarsely amorous ?"

XXIV.

Then of our voyage to the King we spake,
    And all the horrors of that later time,
And how our hearts with fear were near to break
    When we encountered this delicious clime,
    And how that we were guilty of no crime ;
So Rhadamanthus having searched us through
    A long while with those piercing eyes sublime,
At length, persuaded that our speech was true,
Relented of his wrath, and suavely gentle grew.

XXV.

And smiling, warned us that one man's offence
    Against their innocent island-polity
Would be enough to make him drive us thence,
    However pure and still the rest might be ;
    Then, lifting up his voice, declared us free ;
Whereat the chains fell straightway from each limb,
    And all the strange fair faces we could see
Were smiling through the shadows deep and dim,
And each of us was touched by one who greeted him.

XXVI.

And as I stood abashed and flushed, one came
    Who took my hand within his grasp and said,
" Wilt thou that I should call thee by thy name,
    Stranger? my name among the holy dead
    Was Myron, and for home and Greece I bled."
I answered him, and then with hand in hand
    We downward went, I following where he led,
To view the splendours of that magian land,
By beauty so caressed and by such odours fanned.

XXVII.

My tall companion was of aspect grave,
    His features moulded in a form severe,
The locks that round his forehead loved to wave
    Were like an autumn leafage, richly sere ;
    Stern was he, but the trembling heart of fear
Took comfort at the light in his young eyes ;
    Little he said, but spoke out firm and clear,
As one whose hands had taught him to be wise,
And from his robe I marked a dust of marble rise.

XXVIII.

So, each by his own guide, we all were brought
   Into a palace where the heroes sate,
And airy ministrants more swift than thought
   Took off the garments of our former fate,
   And clothed us in thin purple robes of state ;
Then washed our feet in bowls that smelt of myrrh,
   While to the couches where we lay and ate,
On printless feet that made no sound or stir
Came bearing food and wine each gentle minister.

XXIX.

The banquet done, with Myron at my side,
   I wandered out to see the town at ease ;
It hangs above a champaign green and wide
   Close moulded by the tumbling azure seas ;
   Across the fields of flowers a fresh'ning breeze
For ever lifts the glowing atmosphere ;
   Within that city fruits and blossoming trees
Ripen and bud with leafage never sere,
And burn in tender green down many a courtway clear.

XXX.

At topmost of the town a stately hall

    Lets through its portico the clear blue light ;

Hither at noon of day the townsmen all

    In public gatherings take their chief delight,

    And wrangle till the dewy fall of night ;

To Artemis the island-peoples pray,

    Or dance in chorus when the moon is bright,

For where the Stoa lifts its pillars gray

Her statue crowned the street, a beacon far away.

XXXI.

And Myron's work it was, in glowing bronze ;

    Beneath the figure stood the sacred name ;

Serene she seemed as when her godship dons

    The woodland dress that wrought Actæon shame ;

    One hand she held her bow in, and the same

Pressed back her foolish hound ; the other passed

    Behind her neck to lift one shaft of flame

Out of her quiver ; from her eyes she cast

A glance to outstrip in speed the quarry flying fast.

XXXII.

All this and more my grave companion showed ;
    The fountains pulsing in each street and square,
The marble dyke through which the river flowed,
    The temples of the immortal gods of air,
    And their clear-carven images and fair ;
The bright Lyceum to Apollo vowed,
    Where many an athlete strove, shining and bare,
Vast halls from which a noise of tambours loud
Came moduling the dance of footsteps in a crowd.

XXXIII.

No night there is within that island fair ;
    But when the twilight threw its pearly veil
Across the azure of the blinding air,
    And far away to sea each twinkling sail
    Was lightly dyed with crimson faint and pale,
And all the world grew like an opal-stone,
    Fit for the prelude of the nightingale,
Tall Myron turned and said " The day is done,
'Tis time that each of us to his own home was gone."

F

XXXIV.

With that we left the town and climbed the hill,
    Along a path that led through orchard-slopes,
Fenced from the browsing creatures' wanton will
    By thornless cactus, set to mar the hopes
    Of idle goats and truant antelopes ;
From all the branches flowers of radiant hue
    Hung down in long festoons and flying ropes ;
Through which with labouring flight a dusky crew
Of strange sweet songsters passed and warbled as they flew.

XXXV.

At last we took a path high up the steep,
    That brought us out before a house of stone ;
This dwelling looked out eastward o'er the deep
    And heard the loud waves' rounded monotone,
    Too sweet and far that, like a human moan,
Their sound should breed a conscious melancholy ;
    Around it spread a garden green and lone,
Given up to insects fair and blossoms wholly,
With beds of sacred herbs, rue, balsam, vervain, moly.

XXXVI.

"This house is thine," said Myron, "all the while
 That thou art with us." At the open door
There sat a woman with a weary smile,
 Spinning, and gazing down upon the shore,
 Where skiff by skiff came landwards evermore,
As though she looked for one that never came.
 About her arms and down along the floor
The masses of her hair in golden flame
Fell, shedding round a light no shadow of night could tame.

XXXVII.

I watched her in deep silence, for her eyes
 Troubled my pulse with beauty; but we stirred,
And as she turned, I saw the soul arise
 Within her, and the bliss of hope deferred;
 Her noble arms she spread without a word,
A living colour glorified her face,
 And, ere a sound from those fine lips I heard,
Most virgin-like and with a queenly grace,
She rose and locked my form in her divine embrace.

XXXVIII.

Long time I hung in that ambrosial dream,
    And when I waked, I found there none but she ;
Slowly our arms untwined, like some twin stream
    That parts at last in hastening to the sea,
    But knows that soon united it must be
For ever ; as I waited flushed and dumb,
    Across the threshold-stone she passed from me,
Then turned with passion-laden eyes that swum,
And held the curtain back, and smiled, and whispered
    "Come !"

XXXIX.

In such beatitude our days passed by,
    So that the wintry wave we quite forgot,
Nor ever recollected with a sigh
    That boreal country where our sires begot
    Children predestined to a weary lot ;
Beauteous and young we grew, and fit to tread
    Beside the immortal shapes that faded not
In this old island of the lovely dead,
Our minds on glorious dreams and fair romances fed.

XL.

And Myron was my counsellor and guide,
    Who taught me patiently all sacred lore ;
With him I loved to climb the mountain-side,
    Or ride along the margin of the shore,—
    In his wise voice contented evermore ;
Swift through the waves our racing limbs we flung,
    Chased the wild roe across the moorland hoar,
Or, braced for speed, above the footline hung,
In those Olympian games, by lyric Pindar sung.

XLI.

So I and so my former shipmates lived
    Lighthearted as the summer birds that sing ;
If ever in our thoughtful hearts revived
    The solemn warning of that ancient king,
    We smiled, for we were pure in everything ;
Guiltless we moved under his easy yoke,
    Safe in the shelter of his kindly wing,
Nor ever seemed we tempted to provoke
The wrath that on the heads of impious sinners broke.

XLII.

But one was there, the stripling of our crew,
 Cynthius by name, a tall and nimble wight,
Most indiscreet he was, though kind and true ;
 In strange adventures both by day and night
 This restless being took his sole delight ;
And oft we quaked to mark his aspect sly,
 As hand on hip, deep in the evening light,
He taught those townsfolk with an earnest eye
Of things that never were in earth or sea or sky.

XLIII.

Little he loved the quiet Dorian ways,
 To plastic beauty he was somewhat blind ;
The luscious stillness of those blissful days
 Hung like a cloud upon his cheerful mind,
 Nor pleasure in processions could he find ;
Nor blew the flute, nor plucked the lyre-string tense,
 No fillet round his temples would he bind,
But lashed the poets for their lack of sense,
And rated with his tongue the athlete's indolence.

XLIV.

Yet was he, for all this, the chief delight
    Of racer, bard, artificer and sage,
Who clustered round their captious favourite,
    And smiled to hear the youthful stoic wage
    Fantastic war against a nobler age ;
But we, who knew him best, shuddered to see,
    Like some fierce creature in a feeble cage,
His twinkling eye, grown restive, long to be
Alert on some new scheme of daring devilry.

XLV.

Deep in the boscage, high above the town,
    Some ancient king has cleared a cirque of grass,
So large that many guests can sit them down,
    And stretch their limbs and drain a joyous glass ;
    From this fair banquet-hall of leaves there pass
Winding arcades amid the sparser trees,
    And, after feasting, many a lad and lass
May tread these paths in noisy twos and threes,
Lost and regained to sight in verdurous slow degrees.

XLVI.

And daily at the hour that brings the dew
    We gathered there with guests of stately mould,
Once known to sight by such as wandered through
    The Dorian valleys in the age of gold,
    All young as gods, yet all divinely old ;
With these we lay on couches of cool moss,
    While round us waves of wondrous converse rolled,
On which our mortal spirits seemed to toss
Like some frail shallop borne where ocean-currents cross.

XLVII.

But while they spake and wrangled of the wars,
    I marked that Helen sat and only smiled,
Nor glanced aside to mark the flushing scars
    Of heroes whom the grape made nobly wild ;
    Like a ripe rounded peach, downy and mild,
Her cheek lay cool under her watchful eye,
    And Menelaus by her calm beguiled,
Shouted the old Hellenic battle-cry,
And laughed and swung his cup to see the Trojans die.

XLVIII.

But soon I marked that Cynthius ceased to fret,
　　And lost the bright impatient glance he had,
So we, rejoiced to think he could forget
　　His mundane pleasures as a mortal lad,
　　In this new birth grew confident and glad ;
His slim and personable form was seen
　　Each evening at the feast, when we were bade,
Most gravely hastening o'er the shaven green,
To take the seat that brought him nearest to the Queen.

XLIX.

And when the talk grew hottest of the fight,
　　And maids and boys had leave the feast to quit,
Helen and he would rise in all men's sight,
　　To wander in the forest glades, and flit
　　Around the circle in a pensive fit,
No harm being thought, where all could see them plain
　　Deep in the shadow, and through the heart of it,
As through the shafts of the straight summer rain
We see the bending woods and waves of shining grain.

L.

So now we seemed secure of endless joy,
    And quite forgot the sword above our head,
Nor dreamed that sin of one man could destroy
    The innocent quiet of the lives we led ;
    One morn I rose up timely from my bed,
And, wandering through my garden o'er the sea,
    Paused, full of marvel, as with all sail spread,
A fleet below me scudding on the lee
Seemed banded in pursuit of some swift enemy.

LI.

And far before them on the round sky's rim
    I saw a pinnace ploughing through the main,
And though the foamy air around was dim,
    I marked two figures that the plunging strain
    Of the loud breaker struck and shook amain,
So that the sun-bright hair of one of these
    Broke from the fillet where its coils had lain,
And blew around her in the salt-sea breeze
Or fluttered thread by thread across her quivering knees.

LII.

But more and more their crazy bark began
    To sway and toil within the labouring deep,
And faster ever the pursuers ran
    Like wolves upon a lost and foolish sheep,
    Made swifter still to see their quarry creep ;
The mainmast of the boat snapped in the wind,
    I saw the master in his anguish leap,
And the loose canvas from its wreck unbind,
Then sink with hanging hands as one to fate resigned.

LIII.

And on they swept ; but I, oppressed at heart,
    Turned to my own familiar door, and spake
To her who loved me ; and I saw her start,
    Troubled, as one that dreams and would not wake ;
    But soon my anxious voice had power to break
The tissue of light dreams, and she arose ;
    Smiling she came, and for her slumber's sake
Craved sweet excuse, the rosy-tinted snows
Upon her cheeks still flushing from her pure repose.

LIV.

I tried to smile ; but prescience and despair
    Weighed on me with a keener pain than death ;
Beneath the river of her rippling hair
    I wound my arms, and fed on her sweet breath,
    Teaching her lips the secret that he saith
Who could not pour his heart out otherwise ;
    But waits that love may see he sorroweth,
And read the story at his brimming eyes,
And on his breaking heart grow pitiful and wise.

LV.

So she divined that all was done at last ;
    The pleasant mornings that we sat together
Under the deep pomegranate-tree, and cast
    Its unripe fruits far down our slope of heather ;
    The starry nights of high untroubled weather
When through the trees we wandered hand in hand ;
    Watching the ghostly birds of drooping feather
That made a singing glory through the land,
Or with our twining arms each other's bosom spanned.

LVI.

Then rose a clamour at the stricken gate,
    And in there rushed on us an angry crowd ;
" Too late to fly !" they said "too late ! too late !"
    And railed on me in accents vague and loud ;
    Over her knees one moment's space she bowed,
Then stood upright and faced them at my side,
    Until, like hounds a master's voice hath cowed,
That horde fell back, and when their shouts had died,
Their captain to my voice in quavering tones replied.

LVII.

The curse was brought by that most wanton hand
    Of Cynthius ; he, with foolish love enflamed,
Had striven to steal in secret from the land
    Bright Helen, of her sorceries unashamed ;
    The careless shaft thus in the darkness aimed
Had stricken all strangers in the happy isle ;
    Cynthius had pleased his own wild heart untamed,
And now to chasten his unholy guile
The King must drive us thence as men abhorred and vile.

LVIII.

They urged us on, and pushed us to the town ;
　　At every path fresh fugitives we met,
For to the sea-board all were hastening down,
　　Some laughing, some with faces hard and set,
　　Some on whose cheeks the starting tears were wet,
While as we passed the Stoa void and wide,
　　Myron, with eyes not fashioned to forget,
Darted between our captors to my side,
And silently we passed down to the water-side.

LIX.

There dead upon a scaffold Cynthius hung ;
　　Our own black ship was moored against the quay,
And underneath that body as it swung
　　They forced us with a swift discourtesy
　　To climb her sides, hoist sail, and put to sea.
But Myron and my lost beloved stood
　　Tall, pale and silent, watching us, till we
Passed far away upon the glimmering flood,
And round us broke a light of vengeance and of blood.

LX.

Then swiftly through that crimson atmosphere
    We hastened, with no help from wind or oar,
While sorrow pierced us, and the pangs of fear
    O'erpowered our mortal spirits more and more,
    Despair behind us and the storm before ;
With that into the realm of gloom we fled ;
    A tempest broke us like a sullen shore ;
And stunned with awe and hopeless as the dead,
Through the loud zone of night our elfin vessel sped.

A BALLAD OF THE UPPER THAMES.

C

A BALLAD OF THE UPPER THAMES.

I.

AH ! what a storm of wind and hail !
　Another quart of Witney ale,
　　We'll test the cellar's mettle,
And Emma, of her work deprived,—
Our Hebe at the " Rose Revived,"—
　　Shall serve us in the settle.

II.

The mowers from the field shall stray,
The fisher from the lonely bay
　　Shall leave his pool forlorner,
The snooded, shy dock-gatherers too
Shall lift their skirts of dusky blue,
　　And line the chimney-corner.

III.

And through the gusts of whirling rain
The cuckoo's voice may call in vain
    From boughs and steaming thickets ;
We'll listen to the jerking crock,
The ticking of the eight-day clock,
    The chirping of the crickets.

IV.

Until some topic, lightly sprung,
Unloose the timid rustic tongue
    To news of crops or weather,
And men and women, touched to speech,
Respond and babble, each to each,
    Till all discourse together.

V.

Until the wonted ale-house chat
With knotty points of this and that,
    And heat of Whig and Tory,

Resolve into the single stream
Of one old man's disjointed theme,
    An ancient country story.

VI.

I sit and watch from out the pane
The silvery Windrush through the rain
    Haste down to join the Isis,
Half listening to the simple tale
That winds along, thro' draughts of ale,
    On to its measured crisis.

VII.

Or watch the head of him who tells
These long-drawn rural miracles,—
    His worn old cheek that flushes,
His eye that darts above his pipe
Keen as the flashing of a snipe
    Through beds of windless rushes.

VIII.

He tells,—for this was long ago,
The winter of the heavy snow,
  And none but he remembers,—
What fate in love to George befell,
The keeper up at Stanlake Well,—
  Then stirs the fragrant embers,

IX.

Then starts anew :—" When I was young
More champion Berkshire men were flung
  By George in wrestling matches,
Than sacks of wheat could stand a-row
Inside yon shed, or martens go
  To build within these thatches.

X.

His back was like a three-year ash,
His eye had got the steady flash
  That's death to hare or pheasant ;

And when he walked the woods at night
The tramps would take to sudden flight,
   To meet him was not pleasant.

XI.

But still he held himself aloof
From every friendly neighbour's roof,
   Nor chatted in the village ;
The farmers called him proud, for he
Could little in their children see
   But imps brought up to pillage.

XII.

At harvest-home and country dance
He gave the beauties just a glance,
   The calmest of beholders ;
The lasses failed his pulse to move,
Till suddenly he fell in love
   Right over head and shoulders.

XIII.

He went to buy a dog one day
At Inglesham, and on the way
    A sudden snow-storm caught him ;
His path he lost ; at length a lane
Down which the north wind swept amain
    Straight into Lechlade brought him.

XIV.

Within the parlour of the inn,
Snug from the driving frost and din,
    He sipped his gin-and-water,
When like a well-tuned instrument,
Close by him, singing, Mary went,
    The landlord's rosy daughter.

XV.

Her voice, before he caught her face,
Bewitched him with its joyous grace,
    But when he saw her features,

Like any running hare shot dead
His heart leapt suddenly, and his head
    Was like a swooning creature's.

XVI.

He rose and stood, or tried to stand,
He clutched the table with his hand,
    Until she went out, singing ;
Then, sitting down, and calm again,
He felt a kind of quiet pain
    Thro' all his pulses ringing.

XVII.

At first he scarcely knew that this
Strange ache made up of grief and bliss
    Was love, his fancy thronging ;
For Mary's image night and day
From his tired eyelids would not stray,
    But wore him out with longing.

XVIII.

And all that winter and that spring
The very least excuse would bring
 His steps to Mary's presence ;
He'd sit for hours and try to smile,
Yet look as grim and dark the while
 As any judge at sessions.

XIX.

But Mary with her cheerful eyes,
Like hearts-ease where a dewdrop lies,
 And lips like warm carnations,
Laughed, bridling up her sunny head
When jokes and sly remarks were made
 By neighbours and relations.

XX.

So things went on till limes in June
Dropped honey-dust, and all in tune
 The elm-trees rang with thrushes ;

'Tis sweet, when, fed by showers of May,
Through lily-leaves and flowers that sway,
　　The brimming river flushes.

XXI.

The town one evening seemed to keep
A quiet sort of twilight sleep,
　　Hushed, scented, calm and airy ;
And George, who rode across from far,
Found no one sitting in the bar
　　But smiling mistress Mary.

XXII.

Long time he sat and nothing said,
But listened to the chatting maid
　　Who loved this evening leisure ;
It was so dreamy there and sweet,
And she so bright from head to feet
　　He could have wept for pleasure.

XXIII.

His beating heart, that leaped apace,
Took comfort from her smiling face
    That pertly seemed to brave you :—
" If you don't mind a keeper's life,
I wish you'd come and be my wife,
    For no man else shall have you."

XXIV.

She started, turned first white, then red,
And for a minute nothing said,
    Then seemed to search and find him ;
"Good night," she answered, short and straight,
" I had no notion 'twas so late,"
    And shut the door behind him.

XXV.

The threshold pebbles seemed to scorch
His feet ; he leaned against the porch,
    And tore the honey-suckle ;

Up to the window-pots he sighed,—
Then from one casement, opened wide,
   He heard a kind of chuckle.

XXVI.

So, mad with love and sick with rage,
He swore his passion to assuage,
   And by his death abash her ;
He ran three miles from Lechlade town,
Then threw his hat and cudgel down,
   And plunged in Kelmscott lasher.

XXVII.

The moon on Eaton Hastings Wood
Turned white, as any full moon should,
   To see a drowning keeper,
And twice he sank, and twice came out,
But as the eddies whirled about,
   Each time he sank the deeper.

XXVIII.

Now Mary's brother kept the weir,—
A merry lad, a judge of beer,
    And stout for twenty-seven ;—
It chanced that night he smoked at ease
Among his stocks and picotees
    Beneath the summer heaven.

XXIX.

He dashed across the seething din,
Thrust all the piles and rimers in,
    And stopped the weir's mad riot ;
Then rushing to the reedy strand
Swam out, and safely dragged to land,
    Poor George, now white and quiet.

XXX.

Long time before the doors of death
The little fluttering of his breath
    Seemed taking leave for ever ;

His pulse was gone, his cheek was blue,—
But by degrees they brought him to,
　　And bore him from the river.

XXXI.

Now when next day the news went down
The streets and lanes of Lechlade town,
　　It brought much consternation ;
And as the tale the gossips shared
They duly one and all declared
　　The death a dispensation.

XXXII.

How fortunate he showed in time
His selfish aptitude for crime,
　　His passions thus revealing !
Much ill of the deceased was said ;
But when they knew he was not dead,
　　A change came o'er the feeling.

XXXIII.

Then Mary, who had sobbed and cried,
Grew confident and laughing-eyed,
    While all the town grew graver ;
She warbled like a happy bird,
Nor ever made as though she heard
    The names the neighbours gave her.

XXXIV.

For now they all agreed that she
Was much more criminal than he,
    Was pert, and stony-hearted,
That on her head his blood would lie,
Since he was almost sure to die
    From this cold hussey parted.

XXXV.

But still she warbled ; till one day
When every neighbour had her say
    And each spoke somewhat louder,

She stood right up behind the bar,
For all to hear her near or far,
   Nor could a queen look prouder.

XXXVI.

" If any one that's here to-day
Is going over Stanlake-way,
   I'd have him know for certain,
It's not the way to win a wife,
To hang around, and plague her life,
   And peep behind the curtain.

XXXVII.

" Nor after loafing half-a-year,
And blushing when he calls for beer,
   To shout the question at her,
When mother's lying ill in bed,
Awake, and listening overhead,
   And wondering what's the matter.

XXXVIII.

" Men stalk a girl as with a gun,
And if she turns and tries to run,—
　　Their patience all abated,—
They rush and drown themselves for spite,
To punish people whom they might
　　Have won, had they but waited.

XXXIX.

" My brother should have left him there,
Since plainly all his load of care
　　Is more than he can carry ;
In future he may wooing go
To Witney or—to Jericho,—
　　But me he'll never marry."

XL.

The neighbours all were sadly shocked ;
The maiden at their scruples mocked,
　　As through her work she hurried ;

She sang aloud; and yet 'tis said,
That afternoon her eyes were red,
    Her temper crossed and flurried.

XLI.

But out, alas! for maidens' oaths!
When Love puts on his Sunday-clothes
    In vain their hearts are chary;
Before three months had gone about
The Lechlade bells were pealing out,
    And George was marrying Mary.

XLII.

They bought the " Starling and the Thrush "
Just out of Bampton-in-the-Bush,
    And long they lived together;
For many a cheerful day they throve
Contented in each other's love,
    Through sun and stormy weather.

XLIII.

In Bampton Churchyard now they lie,
Their grave is open to the sky,
    No tombstone weighs above them,
But pinks and pansies in a row,
And mignonette, and myrtle show
    That still their children love them."

XLIV.

The old man, sipping at his ale,
Wound up the ending of his tale,
    As dryly as he started,
Shook out the ashes from his pipe,
Then gave his old thin lips a wipe,
    And rose, and slow departed.

XLV.

For, lightened of their load of rain,
The great loose clouds, grown white again,
    Down in the west were blending ;

While high o'erhead the sun rode through
A radiant plain of sparkling blue,
   His noon-day throne ascending.

XLVI.

The Windrush beamed, like polished steel ;
The lark, in mounting, seemed to reel
   With airs too sweet to utter ;
The roses shook their laden leaves,
The martins underneath the eaves
   Began to peep and flutter.

XLVII.

And so, dissolving in the sun,
Our rustic synod, one by one,
   Stole out to work-day labour ;
The fisher found his lines and bait,
Nor would the brown haymakers wait
   To pledge the chattiest neighbour.

XLVIII.

The women rose, among the fields
To reap what the rank margin yields,
   Tall seeded docks that shiver ;
We, loth to leave the " Rose Revived,"
Went last, although we first arrived,
   Down to the brimming river.

MISCELLANEOUS POEMS.

TIMASITHEOS.

O FOR the gift to rise in full degree,
    Not like the showy fungus of a night,
But fed with soft delays, a branching tree !

Where now Olympia struggles to the light
  All ruin, a sacred city long profaned,
Pausanias found amid the shining flight

Of brilliant statues, all unspecked, unstained,
  One hewed about the face, and marred with mire,
Still standing as by right, but deep disdained ;

And when the curious wanderer would inquire
  Whose beauteous antique shape was soiled and shamed,
None there could tell save one white-bearded sire,

Who answered : " This was one who, never tamed,
   With his swift thews won race on flashing race,
Lightly : and Timasitheos was he named,

" The Delphian, and from Phœbus so much grace
   He had, that all the Arcadian world extolled
His manhood and the glory of his face ;

" And from the lips of Phrynichus out-rolled
   Madness of song, praising his brazen feet,
And tight curls closing like the marigold ;

" And Argive Ageladas, as was meet,
   Master of Pheidias, sculptured him, and set
His statue in the ranks of strong and fleet ;

" And three times at the Pythian games he met
   The athletes in the sinewy lists, and won,
And through the dewy streets and meadows wet

" Went singing, crowned from the pancration,
  To Delphi, in a long procession borne,
And met with songs, his city's dearest son ! "

" Then why," Pausanias cried, " this mien forlorn,
  These injured garments, this dishonoured head,
Of all its light and carven beauty shorn ? "

To whom the old indifferent grey-beard said :
  " 'Twas long ago, before my grandsires' days,
And he who knew our history best is dead.

" But see this dim and grey inscription says :—
  " That ' Timasitheos, traitor to the state,
Lift up with pride and fallen on godless ways,

" ' By his fond physical strength intoxicate,
  Plotted with Kylon, and so meanly fell,
Unstable and the prey of envious fate.' "

Too soon, too much adored ! Ah ! much too well
  He cleft the winds and left the world behind !
Too fatal all the shapely miracle

Of his great limbs in faultless form combined !
  Better, ah ! better far to have been less swift,
More kindred to the earth, less to the wind !

For the gods hate not excellence, but lift
  The strong soul slowly on a great endeavour,
And grace their own belovèd, gift by gift,

And with their sleepless eyes have wit to sever
  Man's lawful joy in power from pride of power,
And hover round the loyal soul for ever ;

But the hot insolent head they hold one hour
  High over the ranks of men, then dash it down,
And laugh to see it kiss the dust and cower.

Let others leap straight to the forest-crown !

   Slow growth, cool saps and temperate airs for me,

And strength to stand when all the woods are brown.

THE CHARCOAL-BURNER.

HE lives within the hollow wood,
  From one clear dell he seldom ranges ;
His daily toil in solitude
  Revolves, but never changes.

A still old man, with grizzled beard,
  Grey eye, bent shape, and smoke-tanned features,
His quiet footstep is not feared
  By shyest woodland creatures.

I love to watch the pale blue spire
  His scented labour builds above it ;
I track the woodland by his fire,
  And, seen afar, I love it.

It seems among the serious trees
  The emblem of a living pleasure,

It animates the silences
  As with a tuneful measure.

And dream not that such humdrum ways
  Fold naught of nature's charm around him ;
The mystery of soundless days
  Hath sought for him and found him.

He hides within his simple brain
  An instinct innocent and holy,
The music of a wood-bird's strain,—
  Not blithe, nor melancholy,

But hung upon the calm content
  Of wholesome leaf and bough and blossom—
An unecstatic ravishment
  Born in a rustic bosom.

He knows the moods of forest things,
  He holds, in his own speechless fashion,

For helpless forms of fur and wings
   A mild paternal passion.

Within his horny hand he holds
   The warm brood of the ruddy squirrel;
Their bushy mother storms and scolds,
   But knows no sense of peril.

The dormouse shares his crumb of cheese,
   His homeward trudge the rabbits follow;
He finds, in angles of the trees,
   The cup-nest of the swallow.

And through this sympathy perchance,
   The beating heart of life he reaches
Far more than we who idly dance
   An hour beneath the beeches.

Our science and our empty pride,
   Our busy dream of introspection,

To God seem vain and poor beside
   This dumb, sincere reflection.

Yet he will die unsought, unknown,
   A nameless head-stone stand above him,
And the vast woodland, vague and lone,
   Be all that's left to love him.

THE DEATH OF ARNKEL.

ACROSS the roaring board in Helgafell,
Above the clash of ringing horns of ale,
The guests of Snorri, reddened with the frost,
Weighed all their comrades through a winter night,
Disputing which was first in thew and brain
And courteous acts of manhood; some averred
Their host, the shifty Snorri, first of men,
While some were bent to Arnkel, some to Styrr.
Then Thorleif Kimbi shouted down the hall,
"Folly and windy talk! the stalwart limbs
Of Styrr, and that sharp goodly face of thine,
All-cunning Snorri, make one man, not twain,—
One man in friendship and in rede, not twain,—
Nor that man worthy to be named for skill,
Or strength, or beauty, or for popular arts,
With Arnkel, son of Thorolf the grim ghost.

Wit has he, though not lacking therewithal
In sinew ; see to it, comrades, lest he crush
The savage leaders of our oligarchy,
Vast, indolent, mere iron masks of men,
Unfit for civic uses ; his the hand
To gather all our forces like the reins
Of patient steeds, and drive us at his will,
Unless we stir betimes, and are his bane."

So from his turbulent mouth the shaft struck home,
Venomed with envy and the jealous pride
Of birth ; and ere they roared themselves to rest,
The chieftains vowed that Arnkel must be slain,
Nor waited many days ; for one clear night
Freystein, the spy, as near his sheep he watched,
Saw Arnkel fetching hay from Orlygstad,
With three young thralls of his own household folk,
And left the fold, and crept across the fell,
And wakened from their first sweet midnight sleep
The sons of Thorbrand, and went on, and roused

Snorri, who dreamed of blood and dear revenge.
Then through the frosty moonlit night they sped,
Warmed to the heart with hopes of murderous play,
Nine men from Snorri's house; and by the sea
At Alptafjord they met the six men armed
With Thorlief; scarcely greeted they, but skimmed
Along the black shore of the flashing fjord,
Lit by the large moon in a cloudless sky;
Over the swelling, waving ice they flew,
Grinding the tufts of grass beneath their sleighs,
So silent, that the twigs of juniper
Snapped under them, sharp, like a cracking whip,
Echoing, and so to Orlygstad they came.
But Arnkel saw them through the cold bright air,
And turned, and bade the three young thralls haste home,
To bring back others of their kith to fight;
So, maddened by base fear, they rushed, and one
Or ever he neared the homestead, as he fled,
Slipped on the forehead of a mountain-force,
And volleying down from icy plane to plane,

Woke all the echoes of that waterfall,
And died, while numb with fright the others ran.

But Arnkel bowed, and loosened from his sleigh
The iron runner with its shining point,
And leaped upon the fence, and set his back
Against the hay-stack ; through the frosty night
Its warm deep odour passed into his brain.
But Snorri and his fellows with no word
Sprang from their sleighs, and met below the fence,
And reaching upwards with their brawny arms,
Smote hard at Arnkel. With the runner he,
Cleaving with both hands, parried blow on blow,
Till, shaft by shaft, their spears splintered and snapt ;
Nor would they yet have reached him, but that he,
Gathering a mighty stroke at Thorleif's head,
Dashed down his runner on the icy fence
And shivered it, while backwards Thorleif fell,
Bending the slimness of his supple loins,
Unwounded.   Then a moment's space they stood

Silent.   Then from the haystack at his back
His glittering sword and buckler Arnkel seized,
And like a wild-cat clomb the stack, and stood
Thigh-deep astride upon the quivering hay,
Raining down thrusts and blinding all his foes
With moony lightnings from the flashing steel.
But Thorleif clambered up behind his back ;
And Snorri, with his shield before his face,
Harried him through the wavering veil of hay ;
And Styrr, like some great monster of the falls,
Swayed his huge broadsword in his knotted fists,
And swept it, singing, through the helm and brain,
And deep sank Arnkel on the bloody stack.

They wrapped his corse in hay, and left him there ;
To whom within the silence of the night
Came that dark ghost, his father, whose black face
Affrights the maidens in the milking-stead ;
And till afar along the frozen road
The tinkling of the sleighs he heard, and knew

That, all too late, the thralls of Arnkel came,

He hung above the body of his son,

Casting no shadow in the dazzling moon,

Cursing the gods with inarticulate voice,

And cursing that too-envious mood of men

That brooks no towering excellence, nor heeds

Virtue, nor welfare of th' unsceptered state.

THE MONASTERY GARDEN.

DEEP in the hollow of the cliffs it lay
 Above, the mountain shouted to the sun,
A thousand riotous runlets streamed away,
 And sped the merry mill-wheels one by one.

It slept within the silence and the shade ;
 Above, from cleft to cleft, in glittering light,
The sun-burned millers and their children made
 A jocund noise of labour and delight.

Its pensive terrace scarcely knew the sun,
 But watched the gleam along the belfry-tower,
And scarcely sighing when the day was done,
 Rejoiced as little at the morning-hour.

Thither I came at twilight ; all day long
 My feet had tracked the river, a line of foam ;

The plaintive angelus rose like a song,

 I hailed the great white house and named it

  " home."

But all was bleak and melancholy there ;

 Beneath the barren wall the vine-leaves lay ;

The stony pathway broadened chill and bare,

 The moaning torrent thundered far away.

Beneath the thread-bare branches of the vine,—

 A shivering vine that yearned for summer lands,—

A marble virgin from her hollow shrine

 Held out the solace of her wasted hands.

So mild she was, so cold, so woe-begone,—

 The tears all frozen in her carven eyes,—

She seemed a monument of tender moan,

 The statue of a grief that never dies.

Behind her, on a sweep of lowlier ground,
  Girt by a hedge of yew, the garden lay :
And she, as though by some magician bound,
  Stood vainly yearning for the golden day.

I turned the creaking latch of the frail gate,
  And stood within the pale monks' garden-plot ;
Harsh herbs were there, and shrubs disconsolate,
  But daisies and the generous rose were not.

An autumn sadness on that garden fed ;
  Prim box and cypress allies quenched the light ;
Gray tufts of rue to sprinkle o'er the dead,
  And thrift was there, and hueless aconite.

Each monk had trimmed and fashioned one pale square,
  But filled it always with the same sad herbs ;
No perfume floats within that sombre air,
  Those ashen leaves no boisterous bee disturbs.

And o'er that scentless garden all day long
   The marble Virgin spreads her stainless hands ;
Untinged by rosy light at evensong,
   And unillumed at matins, cold she stands.

Her consolation had no balm for me ;
   To me she seemed like one poor faltering prayer
Breathed by a prisoned soul that sighs to see
   Life pass her narrow cell and leave her there.

Our Lady of Consolation ! so they name
   This icy maiden with her palms outspread !
From busy haunts of happiness they came,
   And knelt to her for solace, and are dead.

They ring the tuneless monastery bell ;
   The dark-stoled monks pass by her one by one ;
They seek the garden that she guards so well,
   And labour till the hour of toil be done.

A little while, like phantoms of their kind,
    They haunt these echoing paths and terraced ways ;
They know not that her shining eyes are blind,
    And wonder that she heeds nor prayer nor praise.

They tend their barren plots and garden-close,
    Still husbanding their faint and hectic breath ;
Meanwhile below the chill white wall there flows
    The whirling, roaring torrent-stream of Death.

Away ! the cold air gathers like a blight ;
    A madness falls within the falling dew ;
The Virgin glimmers in a ghostly light,
    That thrills the darkening garden-allies through.

Away, away ! high up the mountain-side,
    By loud cascade and chattering stream I fly ;
A glow of sunset floods the valley wide,
    And, as I mount, I catch the gleaming sky.

The warm air moves : the red roofs of the mills
    Burn on the velvet darkness of the pines ;
The odour of the breathing cattle fills
    Light meadows where the crocus shoots and shines.

The giant miller claps his rosy hands,
    And roars a jest above the roaring wheel ;
His daughter laughing at the doorway stands,
    His wife is busy with their evening meal.

Life, life is here, but frost and death below ;
    Hail, genial force of homely rustic ways !
Warm my chilled pulse within thy happier glow,
    And gild the wholesome remnant of my days !

No marble virgin in a mossy shrine,
    No garden clad with flowerless herb and tree,
But Nature in her ecstasy be mine,
    And the wide roseate world of bloom for me.

So shall my youth prolong itself and yield
   Sweet harvest, and the clustering fruits of love,
Deep-perfumed alway like a summer field,
   And fed by shower and sunshine from above.

Nor rot in shade, nor drop its hueless buds,
   But ever, as the happy moments run,
Prepare its sheaves to rise in multitudes,
   All richly garnered when its year is done.

PIERRE-FONTAINE, *Sept.* 1880.

THE SHEPHERD OF THE THAMES.

I.

THOU hast gone back to Arcady once more,
False Shepherd, and hast left me here alone,
Here where the soul of London is one moan,
Here where life breaks upon a dusky shore ;
Ah ! was it wisely done to leave me thus,
For is it not mine the magic crook that makes
The iron cloud pearly and luminous ?
For have I not the charmèd voice that wakes
The black-cap swinging in the osier-brakes,
That stirs her heart until it thrills and sings ?
Ah ! without me, light wanderer, canst thou find
The melting briar that breathes upon the wind,
Or where the shy white orchis waves her wings ?

II.

Ah ! that dark wood above the sparkling Thames,
    Where through the honeysuckle pale and sweet
    We saw the silent river at our feet ;
And pushing downward through the springing stems,
Descended to the twilight cumfrey-beds !
    Dream not that thou canst find that wood again.
Ah ! what a glory streamed above our heads !
Surely for thee no mellowing sunset sheds
    Its radiance through the soft and flashing rain ?
Thou shouldst have waited by the lock for me,
    Or where the streaming roots of crows-foot shine,
    Have shipped thine oars and laid thy boat by mine,
Nor thus have gone alone to Arcady.

III.

Yet if thou must, push on, and let me know
    What foxgloves with imperial foreheads nod
    Down the steep coppice, row by stately row ;
And where the mullein lifts her amber rod.

What willow-herb now fringes the high bank,

    Whence many a time we plunged above the weir,—

Cleaving the limpid pool with sinewy flank,

Till the wrecked water-lily's chalice sank

    Swamped by the eddying flood in deluge drear?

Ah me, push on, and bathe there in the sun,

    And listen to the clacking of the mill,

    And dream that we are lithe young shepherds still,

Nor all our pastoral hour of pleasure done.

IV.

And surely in that cool and fresh arcade

    By willows framed above the shelving bank,

    Between the river and the hemlocks rank,

Thou'lt find the hard prints that our feet once made,

Our racing feet, along the dewy grass,

    What time shy Oreads of the woodlands fled,

Yet paused to watch the white-limbed youngsters pass

Who never more shall skim the turf, alas!

    With pliant feet, and breathless faces red,

K

Nor wrestle in the dappling light of leaves,
    Nor lie, deep slumbering, through the noontide heat,
    Nor in a nightly ecstasy repeat
Their faltering songs beneath the moonlit eaves.

V.

We shall not taste our showery spring again,
    Yet cheerful memory makes it doubly dear ;
    The leaves that had no scent when plucked, are sere,
But smell like roses freshened with the rain.
Perchance if we went back once more, and sought
    That secret hill, that visionary stream,
Which gleam so brightly in the glass of thought,
They might not bring us all the charm they brought,
    They might undo the magic of the dream.
We have grown wise and cold with worldly lore,
    Our weary eyes have learned to dread the sun,
    Ah, tell me, tell me, was it sagely done
Thus to go back to Arcady once more ?

DR. OLIVER WENDELL HOLMES,

ON HIS SEVENTY-FIFTH BIRTHDAY,

August 29, 1884.

SIR,

A S Age by Age, thro' fell Enchantment bound,
    The Heroe of some antient Myth is found,
Wild Rocks about him, at the fierce Sea's Brim,
And all his World an Old-Wives' Tale but him,
His Garments, cast upon th' inclement Shoar,
Such as long since our Grandsires' Grandsires wore,
While all his Gestures and his Speech proclaim
Him great Revealer of forgotten Fame,—
    Such, Oh ! Musician, dost thou seem to be
To us who con th' Augustan Age by thee,
Who hearken to thy Verse, to learn thro' it
How DRYDEN to illustrious ORMOND writ,

Or in thy fil'd and polisht Numbers hope

To catch the Secret of the Art of POPE ;

Ah ! subtil Skill ! Ah ! Bard of dying Fires,

Let us but lose thee, and a Race expires ;

So long as thou dost keep this Treasure thine

Great ANNA's Galaxy has Leave to shine.

Thou who do'st link us with that elder Day

When either QUEENSBERRY made Court to GAY,

Thro' all the Thunders of romantick Times,

Thro' Reefs of monstrous Quips and Shoals of Rhimes,

We've steer'd at last, and, like Ships long at Sea,

Our Latest-Born sail home to Grace and thee ;

Home-ward they sail, and find the World they left

Of all but thee, yet not of thee bereft ;

Still in thy pointed Wit their Souls explore

Familiar Fields where CONGREVE rul'd before ;

Still in thy human Tenderness they feel

The honest Voice and beating Heart of STEELE.

Long be it so ; may Sheaf be laid on Sheaf

Ere thy live Garland puts forth its *Last Leaf;*

As in old Prints, long may we see, in Air,

Thy *Guardian Angel* hover o'er thy Hair ;

Still may the *Table*, where our Fathers sat

To eat of Manna, hold its *Autocrat ;*

Since surely none of all the Blest can be

Home-sick in Heav'n, as we on Earth, for thee.

   And Oh ! whil'st o'er th' embattl'd Crags afar

Thy practis'd Eyes gaze down the Gorge of War,

Where thro' the blinding Dust and Heat we fight

Against the Brazen-Helm'd Amalekite,

At Height of Noon, Oh ! lift up both those Hands

To urge new Virtue thro' our fainting Bands,

And when we feel our Sinews nerv'd to strike

Envy and Errour, Shame and Sloth, a-like,

We'll say 'tis well that, while we battle thus,

Our MOSES stands on high 'twixt Heav'n and us.

SIR,

Your Most Humble, Most Obedient Servant,

EDMUND GOSSE.

APRIL ONCE MORE.

THE sorrel lifts her snow-white bloom
   From green leaves soft and sour,
The wry-neck bids the cuckoo come,
   The wych-elm's all in flower;
That tweet! tweet! tweet! that dusty dew,
   That white star at my feet,
They speak of Aprils past—and you,
         My sweet!

Our wood still curves against the sky,
   And still, all stark and dim,
Our hornbeam's fluted branches lie,
   Along the shining rim;
But ah! within its base of moss
   The rabbits leap and peer,
No footsteps fright them as they cross—
         This year.

When winter shared my hapless plight,

   I bound my heart in frost ;

There was no wealth to vex my sight

   With treasure it had lost ;

But oh ! the buds, the scent, the song,

   The agonising blue—

They teach my hopeless heart to long

         For you !

THE CHURCH BY THE SEA.

I.

THAT spirit of wit, whose quenchless ray
　　To wakening England Holland lent,
In whose frail wasted body lay
　　The orient and the occident,

II.

Still wandering in the night of time,
　　Nor yet conceiving dawn should be,
A pilgrim with a gift of rhyme,
　　Sought out Our Lady by the Sea.

III.

Along the desolate downs he rode,
　　And pondered on God's mystic name,
Till with his beads and votive ode,
　　To Walsingham Erasmus came.

IV.

He found the famous chapel there,
  Unswept, unlatticed, undivine,
And the bleak gusts of autumn air
  Blew sand across the holy shrine.

V.

Two tapers in a spicy mist
  Scarce lit the jewelled heaps of gold,
As pilgrim after pilgrim kissed
  The relics that were bought and sold.

VI.

A greedy Canon still beguiled
  The wealthy at his wicket-gate,
And o'er his shining tonsure smiled
  A Virgin doubly desecrate.

VII.

The pattered prayers, the incense swung,
  The embroidered throne, the golden stall,

The precious gifts at random flung,—
  And North Sea sand across it all !

VIII.

He mocked, that spirit of matchless wit ;
  He mourned the rite that warps and seres :
And seeing no hope of health in it,
  He laughed lest he should break in tears.

IX.

And we, if still our reverend fanes
  Lie open to the salt-sea deep,
If flying sand our choir profanes,
  Shall we not laugh, shall we not weep ?

X.

We toll the bell, we throng the aisle,
  We pay a wealth in tithe and fee,
We wreathe the shrine, and all the while
  Our Church lies open to the sea.

XI.

The brackish wind that stirs the flame,
   And fans the painted saints asleep,
From heaven above it never came,
   But from the starless Eastern deep.

XII.

The storm is rising o'er the sea,
   The long bleak windward line is grey,
And when it rises, how shall we
   And our weak tapers fare that day?

XIII.

Perchance amid the roar and crack
   Of starting beams we yet shall stand;
Perchance our idols shall not lack
   Deep burial in the shifting sand.

GILEAD.

"And I will bring them into the land of Gilead."

OH, who will take my hand and let mine eyes have
        rest,
And lead me like a child into the quiet west,
Until beneath my feet I press the short wild grass,
And feel the wind come shorewards down the granite pass ;
So, fashioned darkly round the mirror of the mind,
The solemn forms I loved in infancy to find
Bent down to shut me in, in billowy solitude,—
Harsh tor and quaking sedge and devil-haunted wood,—
Behind the thin pink lids I should not dare to raise,
Would gather and console the turmoil of my days?

A grain of balm has lain within my scentless breast
Through all these roaring years of tempest,—and shall rest,

A single grain, how sweet! but, ah! what perfumes rise,
Where, bathed by sacred dews, the soul's full Gilead lies!

There, with the sands around, and many a mirage faint
To tempt the faded sight of fakir and of saint,
Cool, with their clump of palms, by wells like crystal pure,
The myrrh-trees of the Lord, the dripping boughs endure.

Oh, lead me by the hand, and I with eyelids close
Will hear the wind that sighs, the bubbling stream that
     flows,
The shrill Arabian sounds of blessed aged men,
And the low cries of weary souls at home again;

Yet never raise my lids, lest all these Eastern things,
These forms of alien garb, these palm-surrounded springs,
Surprise my brain that grew in colder zones of light,
Betray with homeless home my impulse of delight.

But when I think I feel the west wind, not the east,
From drought and chilly blue by soft gray airs released,

I'll bend my hand and touch the country at my feet,
And find the sun-dew there, and moor-ferns coarse and
    sweet,
And the rough bilberry-leaves, and feel the mountain-moss
Stretch warm along the rock, and cross it, and re-cross.

What we loved first and lost in Nature, yet retain
In memory, prized the most, worn to a single grain,
That scene, though wild and far, and acrid with the sea,
Pilgrim of life, is still Gilead to thee and me ;
And there where never yet to break the shadows come
Battalions of the world, with bedlam fife and drum,
There, in the ancient hush, the elfin spirit of sleep
Preserves for child-like hearts a pillow broad and deep,
And in a tender twilight, mystic and divine,
The homely scenes we loved take hues of Palestine.

TO AN ACTOR.

Et jam purpureo suras include cothurno—
. . . Sero sapiunt Phryges.—*Livius Andronicus.*

"THE red cothurnus slowly bind around those
    shapely thighs,
Nor fear the giggling Phrygian race that hastes not to be
    wise !"

Thus darkly in a fragment sang, oracularly sage,
Old Andronicus, eldest bard that trod the Latin stage.

We know not rightly what he meant, but yet may soothly
    guess
His Muse was no vain babbler, but a learned prophetess.

We think across the centuries she dreamed, great mime,
    of thee,
And warned thee of the playwrights small, and mobs of
    low degree.

A London audience moved her scorn, a London farce
  awoke
The anger that so dimly and in such dark music broke.

Then take it to thyself and bind the stately buskin on,
Walk in the large and purple light of ages dead and gone.

A holier presence guard thy steps, an antique air impart
The force of classic beauty to the movements of thine art.

Contrive no tricks to charm the pit, nor bend thy face to win
The raptures of a groundling and the suffrage of his grin.

Behind the scenes, as on the stage, forswear all trivial
  things,
And move as one whose heart believes the noble lines he
  sings.

Let gorgeous shapes of tragedy pass on at thy command,
And leave the Phrygian flutes to thrill the uplands of the
  Strand.

DE ROSIS HIBERNIS.

AMBITIOUS Nile, thy banks deplore
　　Their Flavian patron's deep decay :
Thy Memphian pilot laughs no more
　　To see the flower-boat float away ;
Thy winter-roses once were twined
　　Across the gala-streets of Rome,
And thou, like Omphale, could'st bind
　　The vanquished victor in his home.

But if the barge that brought thy store
　　Had foundered in the Lybian deep,
It had not slain thy glory more,
　　Nor plunged thy rose in salter sleep ;
Nor gods nor Cæsars wait thee now,
　　No jealous Pæstum dreads thy spring,
Thy flower enfolds no augur's brow,
　　Nor gives thy poet strength to sing.

L

Yet, surely, when the winds are low,
    And heaven is all alive with stars,
Thy conscious roses still must glow
    Above thy dreaming nenuphars ;
They recollect their high estate,
    The Roman honours they have known,
And while they ponder Cæsar's fate
    They cease to marvel at their own.

A WOMAN'S KEEPSAKE.

I.

THIS I show you, dearest, this is
    More than just a yellow flower,
This was hallowed by your kisses,
    Severed in a sacred hour,
      Laid by your warm hand in mine,
      And I hold it thus divine.

II.

Where the longest rushes shiver
    With their flower-heads full in June,
Bending o'er the eddying river
    As it modulates its tune,
      In among the reeds alone
      This fair iris-bloom was blown.

III.

Could it be to-day, I wonder?
  For it seems so sweet and far,—
Scarce a man's arm-length asunder,
  Where the reeds and lilies are,
    You and I were floating thus,
    While the blackcap sang to us.

IV.

Suddenly you downward darted,
  Drew the three-winged wonder up,
And I caught it—though I started—
  In my lap as in a cup :
    See ! its scentless leaves express
    Our unspoken happiness.

V.

Blessed flower, whom Death pursuing
  Cannot rob of life for me,—
Thou, whose fluttering papery ruin
  I shall watch with ecstacy,—

Fade, thy memory still will keep
Fresh for me as dew or sleep !

VI.

Thou art buried safe for ever
  In the cassia of his kiss !
Sister-blossoms in the river
  None have such a tomb as this ;
    In their void and hurrying stream
    None can dream as thou shalt dream.

VII.

Over thee a girl shall hover
  Raining tears of deep delight,
Till the image of her lover
  Flash across her inward sight,
    And thy faded leaves unfold
    Their old visionary gold.

THEOCRITUS.

For A. Lang's Translation.

THE poplars and the ancient elms
    Make murmurous noises high in air ;
The noon-day sunlight overwhelms
    The brown cicalas basking there ;
But here the shade is deep, and sweet
    With new-mown grass and lentisk-shoots,
And far away the shepherds meet
        With noisy fifes and flutes.

Their clamour dies upon the ear ;
    So now bring forth the rolls of song,
Mouth the rich cadences, nor fear
    Your voice may do the poet wrong ;
Lift up the chalice to our lips,—
    Yet see, before we venture thus,

A stream of red libation drips
    To great Theocritus.

We are in Sicily to-day ;
    And, as the honied metre flows,
Battos and Corydon, at play,
    Will lose the syrinx, gain the rose ;
Soft Amaryllis, too, will bind
    Dark violets round her shining hair,
And in the fountain laugh to find
    Her sun-browned face so fair.

We are in Sicily to day ;
    Ah ! foolish world, too sadly wise,
Why did'st thou e'er let fade away
    Those ancient, innocent ecstasies ?
Along the glens, in chequered flight,
    Hither to-day the nymphs shall flee,
And Pan forsake for our delight
    The tomb of Helice.

WHERE are you, Sylvia, where?
    For our own bird, the woodpecker, is here,
Calling on you with cheerful tappings loud!
The breathing heavens are full of liquid light;
The dew is on the meadow like a cloud;
The earth is moving in her green delight—
Her spiritual crocuses shoot through,
And rathe hepaticas in rose and blue;
But snow-drops that awaited you so long
Died at the thrush's song.

" Adieu, adieu!" they said.
" We saw the skirts of glory, and we fade;
We were the hopeless lovers of the Spring,
Too young, as yet, for any love of ours;
She is harsh, not having heard the white-throat sing;

She is cold, not knowing the tender April showers ;
Yet have we felt her, as the buried grain
May feel the rustle of the unfallen rain ;
We have known her, as the star that sets too soon
Bows to the unseen moon."

THE SONS OF CYDIPPE.

B Y sacred Argos Polycieitus carved,
　　In Indian ivory and Persian gold,
To Hera, mother of all, dreadful, benign,
A glorious statue in his darkened house.

Straight from her throat ran the pure folds, and fell
In seemly curves about her unseen feet :
The fillets of her lifted head were bound
With broidered stories of the Fates and Hours ;
Sceptre and ripe pomegranate, as was meet,
Her queenly hands sustained, and by her side
The rustling peacock spread his gorgeous train.

For ancient Chrysis, from her wrinkled hands
Letting the torch down fall in obscure sleep,
Careless, not breathed on by the serious gods,

Had touched the old Heræum with white flame,

And like a dream the fabric, full of prayers,

Vows of forgotten athletes, maidens' gifts,

Robes of dead priests, echoes of hymns and odes,

Had glared against the noonday, and was not.

So, nigher to Canathus, on lower ground,

Nearer the bright sea, myriad-islanded,

Argos had built her outraged deity

A nobler fane among those holy trees—

Platans and elms—that drank her virgin spring ;

And all was done, and on this certain day,

From the dark house, shrouded and swathed in cloths,

The dread majestic goddess passed in state

To be unveiled within her own abode.

Then while the people, clustered in the sun,

Shouted and pressed, and babes were held aloft,

At one shrill summons of the sacred flute,

In all her gold-and-white magnificence,

The austere god smiled on her worshippers,
Who suddenly fell silent in their awe.
Then came a shout, and from the woodland road,
Craving a passage through the whispering throng,
Two youths appeared, under a shameful yoke,
Flushed with the sun, and soiled with dust, and bowed,
Who dragged a chariot with laborious arms,
Bleeding and chafed ; and on the chariot sat—
With a thin bay-leaf in her aged hair—
A matron with uplifted eyes elate.

Then while all wondered, and the young men sank,
Breathless and glad, before the glorious god,
The high-priest lifted up his voice, and said :
" Blessed art thou, Cydippe, blessed be
Thy sons who shamed themselves to bring thee here !
Oh, not in vain for Biton, not in vain
For Cleobis, the unfruitful toil, the sweat,
The groaning axles, and the grinding yoke !
Unoiled their limbs, unfilleted their hair,

Unbathed their feet, hateful to maids and harsh ;
But to the gods, sweeter than amber drops
That gush from fattest olives of the press,
Fairer than leaves of their own bay, more fresh
Than rosy coldness of young skin, their stains,
Since like a sacrifice of nard and myrrh
Their filial virtue sanctifies the winds."

Then slowly old Cydippe rose and cried :
" Hera, whose priestess I have been and am,
Virgin and matron, at whose angry eyes
Zeus trembles, and the windless plain of heaven
With hyperborean echoes rings and roars,
Remembering thy dread nuptials, a wise god,
Golden and white in thy new-carven shape,
Hear me ! and grant for these my pious sons,
Who saw my tears, and wound their tender arms
Around me, and kissed me calm, and since no steer
Stayed in the byre, dragged out the chariot old,
And wore themselves the galling yoke, and brought

'Their mother to the feast of her desire,
Grant them, O Hera, thy best gift of gifts !"

Whereat the statue from its jewelled eyes
Lightened, and thunder ran from cloud to cloud
In heaven, and the vast company was hushed.
But when they sought for Cleobis, behold
He lay there still, and by his brother's side
Lay Biton, smiling through ambrosial curls,
And when the people touched them they were dead.

II. P.

THIS virgin soul looked shyly forth, and knew
   The fiery face of Love, and then withdrew,
Just when the spices through its garden blew.

With this one glimpse so full a rapture came,
It shrank from earthly joy as pain and shame,
And passed to God on that first mystic flame.

Dissolved, assumed in ardours so intense,
It rose to heights untouched by mortal sense,
Like some pure cloud of molten frankincense.

And that pale lamp of verse, which God had given
To guide this soul, while o'er life's ocean driven,
Was quenched within the blazing glow of heaven.

INSCRIPTION FOR A FOUNTAIN.

DEEP in the heart of this dim wood
    Our Naiad pours her slender urn,
Nor dreams that round its gathering flood
The fortunes of a world will turn.

WITH A COPY OF HERRICK.

FRESH with all airs of woodland brooks
　　And scents of showers,
Take to your haunt of holy books
　　This saint of flowers.

When meadows burn with budding May,
　　And heaven is blue,
Before his shrine our prayers we say,—
　　Saint Robin true.

Love crowned with thorns is on his staff,—
　　Thorns of sweet briar;
His benediction is a laugh,
　　Birds are his choir.

M

His sacred robe of white and red
    Unction distils ;
He hath a nimbus round his head
    Of daffodils.

A WASTED AFTERNOON IN SUTHERLAND.

AH ! what an azure day !
 Beneath the granite gray
The sulky ferox lay
  And waved a fin ;
Above his surly head
The amber river sped,
Shrunk in its summer bed,
  Limpid and thin.

We heard the eddies lisp ;
Deep in the heather crisp
We lay to watch Canisp
  And Suilven blue ;
Between their crags, behold,
A sheet of polished gold,
Where Fewn drew fold by fold
  Her waters through.

" Hopeless the gray fly's wiles !
Our dusky ferox smiles ;
We have trudged for miles and miles
    In vain, in vain ;
Better the storm that fills
The thunder-coloured rills,
Better the shrouded hills
    And drifts of rain !"

But "No ! ah ! no !" I cried ;
" This lovely mountain-side,
In faintest purple dyed
    And golden gray,
Will live in vision still
When nerves forget to thrill,
When hands have lost the skill
    To play and slay !"

But still he watched the sky
With discontented eye,

For never a cloud was nigh,

    Nor stormy flag ;

Noon fell to afternoon,

Till, like a change of tune,

The delicate virgin moon

    Stepped from the crag.

So, through that sleepy weather,

Our rods and we together

Lay on the springing heather,

    Assuaged at last,

And now, through memory's haze,

Best of our fishing days

Seems just that cloudless blaze,

    With never a cast.

OBERMANN YET AGAIN.[1]

THE light falls pink on yonder granite horn ;
   The pine-tree shadows, lengthening, downward
      run ;
I lie in grass as yellow-stalked as corn,
   And by my side there glitters, scarce begun,
      A flask of bright Yvorne,
      Brisk amber in the sun.

With fall of day the vexing flies have fled ;
   The grasshopper now whets his merry scythe ;
The magpie flirts and chuckles round my head ;
   The lizards flash their shining backs, and writhe ;
      The west is waxing red,
      And I am calm and blithe.

Love, like a purple crocus in the grass,
   Lifts its pale sheath, and flashes by my side ;

And friendship, like the sturdy sassafras,
   Laughs, golden, round the field where I abide ;
      And flowers, like duties, pass,
      Gray, white, and blue, and pied.

All tender sounds proclaim the shut of day ;
   My pulse is cool and scarcely seems to beat ;
Why should such blissful moments e'er decay ?
   Why should the moon approach, the sun retreat,
      When thought is clear and gay,
      And life profoundly sweet ?

Most sad of mystics, see, I shut thy book,
   And let mine eyes upon thy mountain rest ;
Upon those liquid-seeming crags I look
   Where thou didst raise thy solitary breast,
      And, chafing, scarce didst brook
      The unconquerable crest.

Thy nearest solace, Obermann, was found
   Where that white peak soars towards a virgin sky,—

Unconscious ever of man's timid round
    Of tiresome duties that about him lie,
        And the only living sound,
        The eagle's Alpine cry.

I cannot breathe that starry atmosphere,
    Nor feign contempt for man's ephemeral days ;
The eagle's note brings music to my ear,
    Only when lost high up in noon-tide blaze,
        And human hope and fear
        Guide all my human ways.

Yet, O sick soul, that eighty years ago
    Trod these high paths in lonesome wretchedness,
Too dull for tears, and felt around thee grow
    The spider-toils of thought, and less and less
        Could'st e'er redeem the glow
        Of youth's unconsciousness, —

Deem not that all thy sorrows move not me,
    Nor yet that veins which run with coarser blood

Forbid my dole of tribute sympathy ;
    Only permit a mind, perchance more rude,
        Too blithely strung to be
        For such high lassitude.

Only permit that not for me thy moan
    Remain the language of these hills and streams ;
That o'er the clouds which float above thy Rhone,
    That round the peak made classic by thy dreams,
        A happier homelier tone
        Should live in memory's gleams.

I need small circuit for this heart of mine ;
    And, God be thanked, all this enchanted land
Is not a glacier-desert crystalline ;
    What waves of odour beat this little strand
        Of crocus and of pine !
        Thy hand, dear friend, thy hand !

Villard-sur-Ollon.
    Aug. 1883.

LIBER CORDIS.

"O let me love my love unto myself alone."

PALINGENESIS.

I WAS fashioned long ago
In an element of snow,
And a white pair of cold wings
Bore me towards sublunar things ;
Over thought's immense dominions,
Floating on those chilly pinions,
Long I wandered, faint and thin
As a leaf the wind may spin,
And the tossing flashing sea
Moaned and whispered under me,
And the mountains of man's mind
Threw short shadows far behind,
And the rivers of the soul
That still thunder as they roll,
At my cold height streamed and fled
Silent as a glacier-bed.

I was light and gay and bold,
Bathing in the sunset's gold,
Though my forehead's only flush
Came from the aurora's rush,
And my white wrists held on high
Showed no blue veins coursing by.
Through the world a dream I went,
Swathed in a frozen element,
Watching with a temperate breath
All the masque of birth and death,
Pleased to mark around, below,
The currents of emotion flow,
Pleased in my insane conceit
That I had no heart to beat.

But, one morning, as I flew
Higher in the vault of blue,
On a storm's eccentric curve
All my flight began to swerve.
Ah ! my crystal limbs expire

In this new domain of fire !
Ah ! my dædal wings must scorch
In this vast aërial torch,
And my fairy garments made
Of the frost's breath, all will fade !

Shrieking in a robe of pain,
Darkness fell upon my brain.
When I wakened, far away
In a still green dell I lay,
Shivering, naked ; warm within
What was this I heard begin
Throbbing, pulsing, like the sound
Of a hammer underground ?
Then I caught a voice, repeating,
"'Tis thy new-born heart that's beating."

Since that day I have not flown
O'er the radiant world alone :
I am all content to follow

Love round this one mountain-hollow ;

Weak I am, and flushed with feeling

Tender hopes around me stealing ;

Tears between my eyelids creep,

And I waken still to weep :

Often as I walk along

I am agonised with song,

Thoughts of one belovèd form

Lash me like a sudden storm,

And for days I travel wholly

Muffled up in melancholy.

Yet for all this weary pain

I would not be calm again,

Yield the warmth and flush and riot

For my earlier crystal quiet,

Or this burning flesh resign

For those wings and robes of mine ;

Having tasted Life and Breath

And the bitter Fear of Death,

Who could any more endure
That chill æther rare and pure?
Having known the ache of loving,
And the warm veins' stir and moving,
And the yearning hopes that start,
Who would live without a heart?

THE CAST.

IF I could read you like a book,
　　Or like a wizard's glass of old,
I might discover why you look
　　　　So cold.

My fate runs ringing through my brain,
　　I am a fool to love you so ;
Will all my rashness be in vain,—
　　　　Or no ?

Your voice, your presence at my side,
　　Are more than flesh and blood can bear ;
I risk your anger ; I decide
　　　　To dare.

"SPACE TO BREATHE, THOUGH SHORT SOEVER."

D EAR Tyrant, for one moment set me free,
    I faint, I weary of my constant ache,
Thy presence in thine absence seems to make
A harder bondage of my heart to thee ;
Let me forget thee for an hour, and see
    Across the east a peaceful sunrise break,
    Shot with no flames enkindled for thy sake,
Bearing no pleasant pains from thee to me.
Let me forget, that like the wave of light
    That floods the watcher who hath dozed at dawn.
    The memory of thy mouth and hands and eyes
May rush upon me with a new delight,
    Clothing the dewy trees and sparkling lawn
    With all the flush and sweetness of surprise.

THE TIDE OF LOVE.

LOVE, flooding all the creeks of my dry soul,
   From which the warm tide ebbed when I was born,
Following the moon of destiny, doth roll
   His slow rich wave along the shore forlorn,
To make the ocean—God—and me, one whole.

So, shuddering in its ecstasy, it lies,
   And, freed from mire and tangle of the ebb,
Reflects the waxing and the waning skies,
   And bears upon its panting breast the web
Of night and her innumerable eyes.

Nor can conceive at all that it was blind,
   But trembling with the sharp approach of love,
That, strenuous, moves without one breath of wind,
   Gasps, as the wakening maid, on whom the Dove
With folded wings of deity declined.

She in the virgin sweetness of her dream
  Thought nothing strange to find her vision true ;
And I thus bathed in living rapture deem
  No moveless drought my channel ever knew,
But rustled always with the murmuring stream.

I STAND before you as a beggar stands,
 Who craves an alms and will not be denied ;
 Nor shall I cease to wander at your side,
Until I gain this largess at your hands ;
Give me your weary thoughts, your hours of pain,
 Your dull grey mornings, and your hopeless moods ;
 If one sad moment mars your solitudes,
Give that to me, and be at ease again.
Behold, my heart is large enough to bear
 Your burdens, and to rock your heart to sleep ;
Give me your griefs, I do not ask to share
 The golden harvest of the joys you reap ;
Be glad alone ; but when your soul's opprest,
Come here and lay your head and be at rest.

ILLUSION.

COY in a covert of the glossy bracken
My love and I sat warm, enchanted, silent,
And watched one tree against the molten azure ;

Its leaves were fretted gold-work in the sunset,
And on a bough that glistered like vermilion,
A roseate bird of paradise sat preening.

Alas ! my love arose and went in anger :
The east wind blew, and all the sky grew leaden,
The bloom and gloss from off the bracken faded.

And, in the hueless larch I still kept watching,
On one brown branch, caught by the storms and broken,
Still sat and preened a common songless fieldfare.

THE LAPWING.

HOW like that pied and restless bird am I
　　　Called Lapwing from her false and feignèd
　　　　　wound!
Lame on one side she painfully doth fly,
　　Drooping her crest, and circling near the ground;
Such thought she takes but to conceal her brood,
　　Who crowd unseen within a helpless nest,
Nor can rough idlers, though their steps intrude,
　　Win that nice secret from her panting breast;
So I in many songs most deftly hide
　　The tender casket of my heart's rich pain,
Lest one dear name my soul hath deified
　　Be trodden upon by wandering feet profane;
I sing my songs for Love's true priests alone,
And Love must watch my nest when I am gone.

OUR WOOD IN WINTER.

THE circle of the wind-swept ground
    Was paved with beechen leaves around,
  Like Nero's golden house in Rome ;
While here and there in solemn lines
The dark pilasters of the pines
  Bore up the high wood's sombre dome ;
Between their shafts, like tapestry flung,
A soft blue vapour fell and hung.

We paused with wonder-taken breath :
It seemed a spot where frost and death
  Themselves were chained at nature's feet ;
And in the glow of youth and love,—
The coloured floor, the lights above,—
  Our hearts, refreshed, with rapture beat ;
The beauty thrilled us through and through
And closer to your side I drew.

Ah, tell me when we both are old, —
On dismal evenings bleak and cold,
  When not a spark is in the west,
When love, aweary grown and faint,
Scarce stirs the echo of complaint
  Within the sad and labouring breast, —
Ah ! tell me then, how once we stood
Transfigured in the gleaming wood.

And in a vision I shall turn
To see the fallen beech-leaves burn
  Reflected in your lifted eyes,
And so for one brief moment gain
The power to cast aside my pain,
  And taste once more what time denies ;
Nor linger till the dream has fled,
But on your shoulder sink my head.

RESERVE.

AS when there peal along the astonished air
 Joy-bells of some exuberant town at play,
 Laughing and shouting in its holiday,
And blind to apprehension, deaf to care,
One standing in the noisy market-square,
 Pausing an instant, pondering—if he may,—
 Will hear above the riot loud and gay
The vast cathedral-organ boom for prayer;
So when I hold your beauty in my arms
 Above the tumult of the pulse, there rings
 A music welling from diviner things;
Your soul reveals to me her nobler charms,
And in the light that dazzles and disarms,
 My too vain-glorious spirit droops her wings.

ANATHOTH.

I PRAISE the all-watchful sovereignty of Love,
 That his imperial melodies have made
My soul a haunt of echoes, Anathoth.

For through the morning, when the briony-stars
From their green lush entanglement were roused,
Like homeward wishes in a wanderer's heart,
While the late blossom from the blushing crab
Fell, in a rosy storm, down the deep lane,
Fretting the truant kine, when every hedge
Was full of snow-white flowers, campion, wild pink,
Starwort, and dittany, and that fair herb,
Cumfrey, that dotes upon the sylvan Thames,
I walked alone, but with a beating heart
As one late touched by the dear hand he loves,
And still right warm with that companionship,
May walk and dream his sweetheart moves beside.

Yet while the assiduous hedges shut me in,

Like too-persistent guests, and while the turf

Was sparkling with those tender blooms of spring,

I had no heart for service ; but when soon

All sank and faded to the open moors,

And the garrulous cuckoo with his wearisome voice

Vexed me no more, then the large silence brought

Back the rich echo of the name I love.

And when, amid the stunted furze, I caught

Glimpse of those mountain wings, embossed with red,

The shy bright silent bird[s] we watched so long,

My heart breathed full of ecstasy and peace,

And I could worship ; there the rigid lines

Of moorland stretched, harmonious ; there the stream

Sprang, the Scamander of a soul besieged,

By Argive witcheries down to bondage drawn.

I trod the battle-field of my desire,

And here she smiled, I said, and here she sat,

And listened to the brooklet more than me,

And here the grasshopper with strident wings

Leaped at her, and her laughter-echoing shriek
Rang down the fluted valleys one by one ;
And here, beneath this little birchen clump,
A silver shadow on the enormous moor,
I kissed her rounded throat without reproach ;
And here upon the topmost table-land,
Between two dips in the bare crown, we sat,
With wreathèd arms and rosy cheek to cheek,
And scanned the landscape by the unfolded chart,—
I, furtive, mapping rather with fond eyes,
The warm carnations of that delicate neck
Where the curled gold creeps lowest.

                    And, for these
Pure memories of the perfect heart's desire,
I praise and thank the sovereignty of Love,
Since in a tender heart, native to bliss,
These vague reminders of sweet time gone by,—
Thrills of the pulse, reanimated flush
From the light exquisite touch of a loved hand,

The shadow of the dream of such delight
As springs when eye meets eye in sudden flame, —
The memory of a momentary sense
That this sad chasm of isolation, set
Between all souls for ever, has been bridged,
Once, by the unselfish courage of desire, —
Are more than all the creeds and all the schools
By vague and visionary longing led
Have dared to dream or preach to us of heaven.

Ay! more than Heaven indeed; and what of Earth—
Earth which is cold to Love, and blind to Heaven?
This,—that such memories are the mountain-airs
Which stir earth's acrid vapours, that their dream
Brings light at sunrise and at sunset peace,
That time without them would be mad and void,
And ache itself away, and, last of all,
That he who bears no echoes in his soul
From such melodious solitudes as these,
Dying, dies ghastlier than the dog he fed.

WE two have strayed far from the noise of earth,
     By heath and peak, by foam-distracted beach,
   By little ancient towns of foreign speech,
By woodlands where the swinging birds made mirth,
By dusky towns, eyes in the moorland-girth
     Of hills, and in the solitude of each
     Your lovelier soul has bent itself to teach
My soul the lore that follows the New Birth.
I think some fragment of our life must make
     A green oasis in those mountain-snows,
     A sanguine flush across the wild white rose,
A bar of opal where the streamlets break,
     Or in some valley there may bloom, who knows,
One little flower created for our sake?

SAND.

IF thou wert here I should not wander thus,
    Scribbling in aimless mood on the wild sand
    The letters of thy name, to teach the land
From Joyous Gard to Castle Perilous
What love is ours, nor, lest men mock at us,
    Return in haste, to find the breeze has fanned
    The shore, and stirred the surface, like a hand,
With smoothing fingers, light and tremulous.
Alas ! by force of loving I become
    Weak as an eddy in the sandy wind,
    Faint as yon phantom-ruin scarce defined
Against the pale mysterious fields of foam ;
Again along the misty strand I roam,
    Dull, chilly, silent, patient and resigned.

TWO POINTS OF VIEW.

I F I forget,—
    May joy pledge this weak heart to sorrow !
       If I forget,—
May my soul's coloured summer borrow
The hueless tones of storm and rain,
Of ruth and terror, shame and pain,—
       If I forget !

       Though you forget,—
There is no binding code for beauty ;
       Though you forget,—
Love was your charm, but not your duty ;
And life's worst breeze must never bring
A ruffle to your silken wing,
       Though you forget.

If I forget,—

The salt creek may forget the ocean ;

If I forget

The heart whence flows my heart's bright motion,

May I sink meanlier than the worst,

Abandoned, outcast, crushed, accurst,—

If I forget !

Though you forget,—

No word of mine shall mar your pleasure ;

Though you forget,—

You filled my barren life with treasure,

You may withdraw the gift you gave,

You still are lord, I still am slave,—

Though you forget.

CUPIDO CRUCIFIXUS.

ONE Love there is all roseate-flushed and fair—
  This is the love that plucks the fruit of life ;
One Love there is with cypress round his hair,
  The love that fought and fell in bitter strife :
Not that nor this the Shade that comes to-day
  With tender hands to soothe my beating heart,—
But the third Love that gains and gives away,
  And in renouncing holds the better part ;
His eyes are very sweet, and bright with tears,
  Like thine own eyes, my Dearest, wet with love ;
He knows that I am weak, and torn with fears,
  Trembling to say too much or not enough,
He knows that on the verge of hope I stand,
With Death and perilous Life on either hand.

RENUNCIATION.

LOVE feeds upon the fiery trial,
    And hugs the arm that smites ;
I bless you for your stern denial,
    And for my lonely nights.

If you had heaped my flame with fuel,
    And been, as I was, blind,
Time might have proved your favour cruel,
    Your tenderness unkind.

The longing flesh outwears the spirit,
    The body tires the soul ;
By giving, we but half inherit,
    By holding back, the whole.

The world may keep its brutal fashion,
    And crush the rose to death ;
Our ecstasy of virgin passion
    Will scent our latest breath.

I lose you, but I gain, in losing,
 Your very life and heart ;
Of all that makes time sweet, in choosing,
 We chose the better part.

I lose you, but I gain for ever
 More than mere lovers hold ;
I gain your ocean for their river,
 And for their dross, your gold.

Then love me, my Desire, my Wonder,
 Through change of world and weather !
Our hearts may louder beat asunder
 Than when they throbbed together.

APOLOGIA.

I HAVE not sinned against the God of love,
   And so I think that when I come to die,
His face will reach to me, and hang above,
   And comfort me, and hush me where I lie.

Weak am I, full of faults, and on the brink
   Of Death perchance with awe my pulse shall move ;
I am not fit to die, and yet I think
   I have not sinned against the god of Love.

I have desired fame, riches, the clear crown
   Of influence, and pleasure's long-drawn zest,
Yet at all times I would have laid these down
   To please the human heart that I love best ;

Wherefore I hope when I must go my way
    Down that dark doubtful road that mortals prove,
Some one will cheer my shivering soul, and say
    He has not sinned against the god of Love.

SONNETS AND QUATORZAINS.

ON CERTAIN CRITICS.

THERE are who bid us chant this modern age,
    With all its shifting hopes and crowded cares,
  School-boards and land-laws, votes and state-affairs,
And, one by one, the puny wars we wage ;
They charge us with our lyric flutes assuage
    The hunger that the lean-ribbed peasant bears,
    Or wreathe our laurel round the last grey hairs
Of the old pauper in his workhouse-cage, —
Not wisely ; for the round world spins so fast,
    Leaps in the air, staggers, and shoots, and halts, —
    We know not what is false or what is true ;
But in the firm perspectives of the past
    We see the picture duly, and its faults
    Are softly moulded by a filmy blue.

AUGUST.

THE soul is like a song-bird, and must hold
  Its silent August, or its heart would break ;
From the hot rushes of the unruffled lake
No warbler pipes, and where the elms enfold
Blackbird and thrush, no music is outrolled ;
  They wait in solitude and voiceless ache,
  Till, with serenest winds, September wake
The enchanted pipes and winged age of gold.
So with the heart ; and therefore blame thou not,
  Brisk lover, that thy pensive maid is mute,
    Wandering beside thee with a downcast air ;
She is not heedless, nor thy love forgot,
  But passion dons her dreamy autumn suit
    To wake renewed in beauty, freshly fair.

A WOMAN'S AMBITION.

BEAUTY and Strength and Genius, all are thine,
    And I have nothing but the love of these,
  Born with no charming parts, no power to please,
No sovereign skill to make the future mine ;
Yet could I, but for thee, such gifts resign,
    Without a sigh, and from a heart at ease,
  But, dreaming, with my hands upon your knees,
For all these treasures, like a child, I pine.
I would be praised for beauty, that thine eyes
    Might sparkle, knowing this face to be thine own,
And then accept its complete sacrifice ;
    I would be strong, thy shield-bearer to be,
And famous, that the world's loud trumpet blown
    Might prove me worthy to be loved by thee.

WRESTLING WITH THE ANGEL.

IT was not when my enemy had made
   Large progress, and his youth sustained him well,
  But on the solemn morning that he fell
My soul withdrew apart and was afraid ;
And at the door of my bright hopes I stayed,
   And wondered at the sudden miracle,
   And shuddered inwardly, since who could tell
Why my foe's sinew and not mine decayed ;
So, in the peace around, and when men came
   To press my hands and murmur words of praise,
   I shrank abashed, and hid me from their gaze,
Longing to be like Jacob, tired and lame,
But wrestling still with One whose gracious name
   When all the night was past should break in blaze.

TO TERESA.

DEAR child of mine, the wealth of whose warm hair
  Hangs like ripe clusters of the apricot,
 Thy blue eyes, gazing, comprehend me not,
But love me, and for love alone I care;
Thou listenest with a shy and serious air,
  Like some Sabrina from her weedy grot
  Outpeeping coyly when the noon is hot
To watch some shepherd piping unaware.
'Twas not for thee I sang, dear child;—and yet
  Would that my song could reach such ears as thine,
Pierce to young hearts unsullied by the fret
  Of years in their white innocence divine;
Crowned with a wreath of buds still dewy-wet,
  O what a fragrant coronal were mine!

UNHEARD MUSIC.

MEN say that, far above our octaves, pierce
Clear sounds that soar and clamour at
heaven's high gate,
Heard only of bards in vision, and saints that wait
In instant prayer with godly-purgèd ears:
This is that fabled music of the spheres,
Undreamed of by the crowd that, early and late,
Lift up their voice in joy, grief, hope, or hate,
The diapason of their smiles and tears.
The heart's voice, too, may be so keen and high
That Love's own ears may watch for it in vain,
Nor part the harmonics of bliss and pain,
Nor hear the soul beneath a long kiss sigh,
Nor feel the caught breath's throbbing anthem die
When closely-twinèd arms relax again.

PÉRIGUEUX.

To H. T.

THE little southern city, full of light,
    Full of warm light, and coloured like a peach ;
  The river winnowing either chalky beach
With eddying streams from some vine-haunted height ;
Those pillar'd windows hung with kerchiefs bright,
    That rosy bell-tower with its mellow speech
    In liquid bells that murmured each to each,
Those fleecy, full acacias, robed in white !
Ah ! most those warm acacias ! like a tune
    Their odour fell and rose and died away
      All through that noiseless dreamy afternoon ;
Beside the quay you sat and sketched ; I lay
    To watch the trembling breezes lift and sway
      The boughs through which there climbed a shadowy
      moon.

P

THE VOICE OF D. G. R.

FROM this carved chair wherein I sit to-night,
 The dead man read in accents deep and strong,
 Through lips that were like Chaucer's, his great song
About the Beryl and its virgin light ;
And still that music lives in death's despite,
 And though my pilgrimage on earth be long,
 Time cannot do my memory so much wrong
As e'er to make that gracious voice take flight.
I sit here with closed eyes ; the sound comes back,
With youth, and hope, and glory on its track,
 A solemn organ-music of the mind ;
So, when the oracular moon brings back the tide,
After long drought, the sandy channel wide
 Murmurs with waves, and sings beneath the wind.

THE TWOFOLD CORD.

SINGLY we fight against enormous odds,—
    Dulness, and Cowardice, and Fate, and Chance,
    And the wild bowman, purblind Ignorance,
And Heaven with all its lazy brood of gods;
How, then, above the congregated clods,
    Can one man rise, and out of clay advance,
    Alone, against the sleepless countenance
Of that huge Argus-host that never nods?
So must we fall upon the fields of life,
    And bleed, and die? Nay, rather let us twain,
    Marching abreast, against that army move,
Each harnessing the other for the strife,—
    You with my will for helmet, and my brain
        For sword, while I for buckler bear your love.

THE TWOFOLD VOICE.

A DOUBLE voice cries in the spirit of Man,
    As though upon a mortal stage he saw
Apollo's murmuring daughter, crazed with awe,
Change parts, and shout as Clytemnestra can ;
For in the blaze of life he turns to scan
    The dim ghost-haunted face of outraged law,
    And feels the flames rise, and the serpents gnaw
Through the gilt tissue of his hope's bright plan ;
And thus the heavy animal part of him,—
    Never at rest to ponder or rejoice,—
    Sways, blindly shaken by that twofold voice ;
Beneath the axe of Pleasure, void and dim
The dull brain reels, and the vext senses swim,
    Or Conscience thrills him with her piercing noise.

WHEN by the fire we sit with hand in hand,
    My spirit seems to watch beside your knee,
Alert and eager at your least command
    To do your bidding over earth and sea ;
You sigh—and of that dubious message fain,
    I scour the world to bring you what you lack,
Till, from some island of the spicy main,
    The pressure of your fingers calls me back :
You smile,—and I, who love to be your slave,
    Post round the orb at your fantastic will,
Though, while my fancy skims the laughing wave,
    My hand lies happy in your hand, and still ;
Nor more from fortune or from life would crave
    Than that dear silent service to fulfil.

Q

THE FEAR OF DEATH.

LAST night I woke and found between us drawn,—
  Between us, where no mortal fear may creep,—
The vision of Death dividing us in sleep ;
And suddenly I thought, Ere light shall dawn
Some day,—the substance, not the shadow, of Death
  Shall cleave us like a sword.   The vision passed,
  But all its new-born horror held me fast,
And till day broke I listened for your breath.
Some day to wake, and find that coloured skies,
  And pipings in the woods, and petals wet,
  Are things for aching memory to forget ;
And that your living hands and mouth and eyes
Are part of all the world's old histories !—
  Dear God ! a little longer, ah not yet !

D EAREST and most inseparable Friend,
  Why is it that the thought of thee is bound
With one small plot of honey-scented ground,
Through which a murmuring river without end
Flows, while its eddies with the grasses blend?
  Have I been there with thee? Has that low sound
  In thy wise voice a tenderer echo found?
What valley is this towards which my dreams descend?
Is it that corner of your leaguered brain,
  Shut in by high ambitions, and the stress
   Of battling hopes and godlike imagery,
Where you grow hushed and like a child again,
  Shifting your armour for an easier dress,
   To sit an hour and hold me company?

SLEEP.

FROM THÉOPHILE DE VIAU.[G]

I 'VE kissed thee, Sweetheart, in a dream at least,
    And though the core of love is in me still,
    This joy, that in my sense did softly thrill,
The ardour of my longing hath appeased,
And by this tender strife my spirit, eased,
    Can laugh at that sweet theft against thy will,
    And, half consoled, I soothe myself until
I find my heart from all its pain released.
My senses, hushed, begin to fall on sleep;
Slumber, for which two weary nights I weep,
    Takes thy dear place at last within mine eyes;
And though so cold he is, as all men vow,
    For me he breaks his natural icy guise
And shows himself more warm and fond than thou.

A PORTRAIT.

SHE hath lived so silently and loved so much,
    That she is deeply stirred by little things,
While pain's long ache and sorrow's sharper stings
Scarce move her spirit that eludes their clutch ;
But one half-tone of music, or the touch
    Of some tame bird's eager vibrating wings,
    Breaks up the sealèd fountain's murmurings
To storm, or what in others might seem such ;
So, when she lifts her serious lids to turn
    On ours her soft and magical dark eyes,
    All womanhood seems on her, in disguise ;
As on the pale white peacock we discern
    The pencilled shadows of the radiant dyes
And coloured moons that on her sisters burn.

A PLEA.

THE Preacher who hath fought a goodly fight
    And toiled for his great Master all day long,
  Grows faint and harassed after evensong,
And harshly chides the eager proselyte ;
The Sage who strode along the even height
    Of narrow Justice severing wrong from wrong,
    Stumbles, and sinks below the common throng,
In pits of prejudice forlorn of light.
But thou, within whose veins a cooler blood
    Runs reasonably quiet, brand not thou
    With name of hypocrite each sunken brow ;
To every son of man on earth who would
The Graces have not given it to be good,
    And virtuous fruit may break the laden bough.

NOTES.

NOTES.

¹ Page 1. *Firdausi in Exile*. This poem was written as an introduction to Miss Helen Zimmern's excellent prose paraphrase of the *Shah-Nameh*, published in 1883, as *The Epic of Kings*.

² Page 31. *The Cruise of the Rover*. When this ballad first appeared, in the *Magazine of Art*, I was bewildered to find my innocent piece of antiquarianism hotly assailed for its bigotry. The publishers of the magazine were annoyed by letters from indignant correspondents, and one gentleman, a resident of Dublin, wrote to let me know that it would be more than my life was worth to me to set foot in that city. As I have Catholic friends whom I love and respect, and as it might chance to be convenient for me to visit Dublin, I must explain that the sentiments expressed are not those of to-day. I have tried to write in the spirit of an English Protestant,—a provincial Protestant, let us suppose,—of the end of the sixteenth century, many of my touches being in fact suggested to me by the account of his truculent adventures and subsequent sufferings printed by that excellent " Western Gentleman of Tavistock," Master Richard Peeke. I owe something also to *The unfortunate Voyage of the Jesus to Tripoli*, in 1584. Both of these extremely rare and

curious tracts have been reprinted by Mr. Edward Arber. The frontispiece to this volume, engraved by Mr. James D. Cooper from part of a tapestry of 1588, now in the House of Lords, and never before reproduced, gives an exact idea of the clumsy Spanish plate-ships which such pious pirates as my " Rover " considered their proper quarry.

³ Page 47. *The Island of the Blest.* This Lucianic study, now printed for the first time, was written in 1879, and then seen by a few friends. To this fact I owe the honour which Mr. Andrew Lang has done me to inscribe with my initials his treatment of a part of the same theme in *The Fortunate Islands* (*Rhymes à la Mode*, 1884). The lines particularly addressed to me in this beautiful poem I take the liberty of transcribing here, as a comment :—

> *Each in the self-same field we glean*
> *The field of the Samosatene,*
> *Each something takes and something leaves*
>   *And this must choose, and that forego*
> *In Lucian's visionary sheaves,*
>   *To twine a modern posy so;*
> *But all my gleanings, truth to tell,*
> *Are mixed with mournful asphodel,*
> *While yours are wreathed with poppies red,*
>   *With flowers that Helen's feet have kissed,*
> *With leaves of vine that garlanded*
>   *The Syrian Pantagruelist,*
> *The sage who laughed the world away,*
>   *Who mocked at Gods, and men, and care,*
> *More sweet of voice than Rabelais,*
>   *And lighter-hearted than Voltaire.*

Moreover, in the interval between the writing and the printing of my verses, a second Oxford poet, without any relation to Mr. Lang or myself, has gone to the *Vera Historia* for his theme.   I permit myself the indiscretion of saying that the delicate romance called "In Scheria," which is to be found in the anonymous volume by three friends, entitled *Love in Idleness* (Kegan Paul, Trench & Co. 1883), is the work of Mr. J. W. Mackail.

[4] Page 166.   *Obermann yet again.*   Mr. Matthew Arnold does not need my apology for this mild expression of protest, suggested rather perhaps by temperament than by conviction, against a certain aspect of Sénancour's famous book on which Mr. Arnold has not cared to lay stress, and which his blind admirers refuse to perceive. Mr. Arnold's healthy imagination enables him to draw comfort from a melancholy which, as we are apt to forget, has proved a direct incentive to suicide in the case of certain morbid minds, such in particular as Sautelet and Rabbe.

[5] Page 189.   *The shy bright silent bird.*   The Mountain Bunting (*Emberiza nivalis*).

[6] Page 216.   *Sleep.*   The original appears thus in the squat little duodecimo of *Les Oeuvres de Théophile* published at Rouen, in 1632, soon after the death of the unfortunate poet :—

> *Au moins ay-ie songé que ie vous ay baisée,*
> *   Et bien que tout l'amour ne s'en soit pas allé,*
> *   Ce feu qui dans mes sens a doucement coulé,*
> *Rend en quelque façon ma flâme r'apaisée.*
> *Apres ce doux effort mon ame reposée,*
> *   Peut rire du plaisir qu'elle vous a volé,*
> *   Et de tant de refus à demy consolé,*
> *Ie trouue desormais ma guerison aisée.*

Mes sens desia remis commencent à dormir,
Le sommeil qui deux nuicts m'auoit laissé gemir,
   En fin dedãs mes yeux vous fait quitter la place :
Et quoy qu'il soit si froid au iugement de tous,
   Il a rompu pour moy son naturel de glace,
Et s'est monstré plus chaud et plus humain que vous.

CHISWICK PRESS:—C. WHITTINGHAM AND CO., TOOKS COURT,
CHANCERY LANE.